This work is of fiction. The names, characters, places, events, and incidents are either entirely the product of the author's imagination or are used fictitiously. Any resemblance to actual persons, living or deceased, or to actual events, is simply coincidental.

Cover Art Design/Art: Grey Gardener/Get Covers.

ISBN: 979-8-218-57235-8

Terra

A Novel By
Grey Gardener

Edited By
H.Erin

Dedication

To the moments humanity has wasted, the secrets lost, and the secrets kept, buried deep in the pockets of time.

Terra.

WINDEN
DAWN PLAINS
MOUNT ULRICH
EMERALD RANCH
NIMBLEPINE
BROWNCREEK
BRIDGEWATER
HEARTLANDS
HAMILTON
POST OFFICE
WHITLEY RANCH

Kendall.

Orbiting Earth.

The door to the men's cabin slid open just as Kendall sprinted past. Knowing that she was already behind schedule her heart raced. The rest of the crew were spilling out of their cabins uniformed and ready, falling into formation without hesitation. Kendall barely slowed, her footsteps matching the rhythm of the crew as they all moved toward the briefing room. The curved corridor seemed to stretch endlessly ahead, the pressure building as the doorway finally came into view. She couldn't be late again—not for this.

The Dawn, painted in muted shades of gray and black, was unlike any other vessel in the Tech Mundus fleet. a C-shaped cylinder with a central corridor running through it like a vein, connected various compartments in a fluid, uninterrupted pattern. Instead of the typical blocky cargo holds or wings, The Dawn featured modular compartments that could detach and reconfigure depending on the mission, making its adaptability in both combat and exploration unprecedented. Its external plating was a matted reflective stealth alloy that absorbed most light, making it nearly invisible in deep space. The artificial gravity had been increased the last few weeks before deployment as part of the Acclimatization Protocol. Kendall's legs and lungs burned in the stale air of the corridor the longer they walked.

Oliver was the first to the door, and it slid open nearly soundlessly. The crew entered the briefing room together and then split off to take their respective seats. From her chair, Kendall could see the badges of past missions' engineers lined up above the door. She felt the weight of those badges and the people who had worn them. She'd walked under that display so many times before without a second glance, but they seemed to shine brighter today. The weight of their mission, the years of preparation, the perseverance and achievement of all the missions before them, suddenly felt more real. They would be the next to add their achievements to that legacy.

The crew of the Dawn was a diverse group of eight, each bringing unique skills and backgrounds to the mission. The mission was specifically designed to be covert: a secret government operation confidential to the general public. Each

member of the crew had traveled on many different starships before, but the Dawn was different. Normally crewed by fifteen, half of the ship had been cut off to conserve energy, leaving it feeling more like a station.
Now, there were only 8 crew members on board. Everyone stayed on the left side of the ship, which consisted mainly of cabins, a kitchen, 2 sanitary stations, and the library. The bridge lay in the center of the "C", and storage and the single docking bay took up the bottom floors.

Life aboard the Dawn swirled in patterns. The average workday was 13 continuous hours of on-call time conducting experiments, performing maintenance, and training for deployment. Before traveling back in time, the Dawn received its orders daily from Mission Control. Now, they came from Captain Moody. For Kendall, the botanist on board, this usually meant fossilized seed samples and lists of plants to find, collect, categorize, germinate, and prep for transport home. Weekly, she was on the air filtration maintenance rotation and the weekly audit with a different partner each time. She enjoyed these jobs until her turn came around to be paired with Von. He was just so bitter all the time. He couldn't even lighten up to crack a few jokes while they shimmied through the ducting.
Her palms were sweaty as she waited for the others to finish sitting down. This would be their

final meeting before descending to Earth, back to a time when the planet thrived with natural resources—resources their future Earth had squandered. They all knew how crucial the mission was for the survival of their future civilization. Every moment they were gone, starvation and resource depletion threatened the world they knew. Anything they found that could be taken back and successfully grown would buy everyone time.

"Hello," the pilot's mellow voice resonated through the briefing room, emanating from the communicator grids embedded in the walls. "Hello Dawn Crew. I'm pleased to say good day, Captain Moody." Lidia rarely left her quarters, like most Mundus pilots whose time was taken up with the intricate calculations and mapping required for time travel and operating the ship. Their work was critical but often went unnoticed, Kendall thought.

Eva Anderson. Second-in-command, was a tactical expert, excelled in strategy and navigation, maintaining order within the crew, chimed in from another channel. "Storage and resource allocation has been adjusted in preparation for final lockdown. The crew will have ample resources to last the next 3 weeks. Field equipment is now available for assignment," Eva concluded, her voice fading from the communicators.

The briefing room fell silent as the crew absorbed the meaning of the pilot's words. Despite their extensive training and expertise, the notion of embarking on this particular journey felt surreal. Captain Moody nodded gravely, her face stern yet revealing a hint of relief.

"Thank you, Lidia, Eva. Your diligence ensures we are well-prepared.

"Only 2 weeks 'till drop." Kendall and Oliver exchanged a glance, as did the rest of the crew around them.

"First of all," the captain continued, "your equipment and handhelds have been stowed in the main transport vessel. Please be sure to double-check your loadout, but there should still be plenty of space for everyone on board.

At the edge of her vision, Kendall saw Von in the corner, sighing and rolling his eyes. He had been irritated and impatient since they boarded the Dawn, clearly upset at being assigned to yet another months-long expedition. He had just finished the preliminary mission for this same effort and hoped to take some time off, but instead he found himself on the Dawn. He could not get home fast enough.

As Kendall refocused on the debriefing, Captain Moody began to pace.

"There have been few in your shoes. Not many get to travel through time, so stay sharp and stick to your assignments. Lidia made an affirming noise through the communicator.

"I've said this before, but collect anything we might be able to use. We only get one shot." Von raised his hand, his expression blank.

"How do we know this will work, Captain?" Despite the apparent simplicity of the question, it echoed the silent doubts of all present. "We've trained for this. N.I.N.A. of Tech Mundus has years' worth of projections saying this is what we need." She flicked her wrist to summon a holographic display of their trajectory and timeline above her. "Obviously, I can't see the future, but I choose to believe them. She scanned the room. Seeing no further questions, she continued, "Good," and resumed her pacing.

"We only have a few more orbits until we get into position. Use this time for mental preparation and equipment checks. Enjoy your downtime while you can, we won't have much of it when we descend. Let's make history. "Mission debriefing is over, enjoy your meal."

As the first of them stood up to go, the tension in the room eased. They all made their way back down the corridor to the recreation room. It was the largest room on the ship, a spacious twenty-by-twenty-foot area that served as the social heart of the Dawn. Here, the crew would dine, watch programs, and relax together. Oliver and Von arrived first and settled at their usual table and took out their cards. Lighthearted banter filled the room, but each conversation was clearly influenced by the captain's earlier words and each person's thoughts on the upcoming mission.

Kendall made a quick stop to find and do a quick check of her equipment in the transport, running through the checklist in her mind: botanical specimen collection kits, personal safety gear, rations, portable comms. Then she collected her meal and settled into her usual seat, one row over from where Von and Oliver were deep in their card game.

The size of the room meant that even whispered conversations were audible. Privacy was a rare commodity Kendall was hoping to enjoy a little more of, once they deployed.

"All I'm saying is, if they were as confident as they claim, wouldn't we have more ships - or, you know, one fully-manned one?" Von's voice was low, but he knew everyone in the room could hear him.

"Maybe, but think about it," Oliver responded with a shrug, "if they sent a fleet, it would cause a huge uproar. We're the scouts, you know. We come back, coast is clear, then the fleet will follow, you know?" Von cleared his throat roughly and took a swig of his drink.

"Aw, come on, man, it'll be fine," said Oliver.

There was a moment of silence while Von squinted at his cards as if he'd never seen them before.

"You ever heard of a fuckin' Viking, Oliver?" He'd raised his voice to a more normal level.

"Um, yeah. They're…um—"

"Proto-Norwegians, Swedes, and Danes," Terry interjected blandly. "Most were farmers, traders, blacksmiths, and the occasional craftsman." He looked away from the holographic map he'd been reviewing and fixed Oliver and Von with a steady stare, eyes blinking slowly.

"For more reason than one, they took to raiding, raping, and pillaging towns, villages, churches, and monasteries. Most of the places they attacked were along coasts." His right hand drifted up to stroke at his chin, and his gaze lingered on Von, a hint of annoyance flickering across his face. After he'd finished, he slowly turned his attention back to his map.

Terry, an ape and the only non-human on the crew, was their field specialist. More than the rest of them, he'd been trained in history and the sociology of the area they expected to land in as a safeguard should they encounter any native citizens. It was his job to…

Eager to join the conversation, Kendall chimed in, "We're headed to a period where weapons were said to be at their apex of the century. They apparently had extremely powerful weapons that didn't require any electricity at all." Her tone carried a mix of curiosity and skepticism about how such technology could exist.

Oliver, unfazed, casually tapped his hip where his standard-issue energy weapon would normally hang. "Would be cool to see, but since we're not allowed to carry off the ship…" He trailed off as Von cleared his throat again.

"So," he stopped to place a card on the table, "what happens if we get into a situation we can't predict? Or one of us gets sick? They couldn't possibly vaccinate for everything." He flipped a card over, leaning back to survey the table. "What happens if we get stuck here?" He smirked, "How does living the rest of your life with no electricity sound, Oliver?"

Plucking a card from his deck, Oliver tossed it casually onto the table, pointedly avoiding Von's eye. "Oh, you mean no computers, no refrigeration or air conditioning. No reliable water source, modern transportation, not to mention limited communication and non-automated food prep. It'll be a nice adventure." There was more than a hint of sarcasm at the end. Oliver was in his late twenties and the youngest of their group. Nonetheless, he stood out. He towered a full head over the next tallest and had wide shoulders and arms that showed he spent long hours in the gym. His background as a marine had gotten him assigned to this mission, and he was both their chief engineer and their most weapon-proficient, but it was no secret that he wasn't too fond of the outdoors.

A brief silence settled over them before Kendall broke back in. "But that's why we're here. People are scrambling for energy and food; we don't want to revert back to times like these."

When the silence began to border on awkward, she chimed in again. "Plus, our studies indicate that by around 1815, people should start to discover," she raised her hands and gave them a little shake to imitate shimmer, "steamboat travel."

Oliver turned to her, and his smile was back, "If that's even real." They shared a laugh, and the tension quickly dissipated. They all returned to their respective activities, Kendall to her food, Von to his brooding, and Oliver to losing at cards.

"Yeah, yeah. We'll see what's real." Von muttered not quite under his breath.

Terry left to do his own checks and turn in before the game ended. Kendall stuck around to hear Oliver complain about how he'd never beat anyone at cards, cleared her place, and went off to relax in her bunk before bed.

Von was the only one who didn't leave, and Kendall saw him wander over to the large artificial window that dominated the far wall of the community room, where the ship projected images of the surrounding space.

It occurred to her, as the door to her room closed behind her, that in all the weeks they'd spent on the ship together, Kendall had never bothered to ask Von why he seemed to be so against the concept of the mission and had accepted the post anyway. She knew why all the others had, from

Oliver's desire to make a name for himself to Moody's enthusiastic, absolute belief in its importance. It irked her a bit that she might've been able to find some common ground with Von and had missed it because of a simple oversight but reasoned that there was still plenty of mission left. Surely, with all the time on deployment without any entertainment but her plants, starting a conversation with Von would eventually become preferable to boredom. When the crew went to sleep, the only sounds on the Dawn were the humming of the life support systems. Most of the crew maintained the usual sleep cycles, although referencing terms like night and day aboard a ship with no simulation programming was considered taboo. When she lay down, though, Kendall felt like, if she had a window, the sun might still be up. Her thoughts were a jumbled mix of how tired her body felt and how quickly her mind still ran.

An immeasurable amount of time later, she was still lying away when the distinct sound of boots clicking against the metal floor echoed rapidly from the hallway. Probably Moody, Kendall mused, knowing the impending deployment meant hours of work for the captain.

A frantic knocking erupted, echoing in the small space, then the door slid open.

"Come with me." It was Eva, her voice low and commanding. Her face betrayed nothing, but when Kendall didn't move right away, something flickered across it. Kendall couldn't remember the last time she'd seen Eva in person. Usually, she was sequestered in her quarters doing whatever pilots did.

"Ah, come on!" Oliver's voice sounded behind her, and Kendall could see that the men's cabin door was open and he had his head bent to fit through it. "We're supposed to be resting. The extra gravity takes so much out–"

"Code Blue, dickhead. Let's go!"

"A Code Blue?" Kendall's heart raced. Eva huffed and turned back to her, gesturing for Kendall to get dressed.

"I just audited the last security report. An extra badge scanned through one of the doors on the lower level. Not one of ours."

Juelz
1872

"The Dice? Be here at 7pm., feller." Juelz said nothing but gave a nod in response, turned, and made his way out of the train station.

As he strode down the main road, the click of his boots against the cobblestone mingled with the distant hum of the town's nightly activities. NimblePine, with its strange glow and the unexpected scent of baking bread washing away the sour scent of the streets, always managed to surprise him. Nestled at the edge of the frontier, the town blended the old with the almost mystical, its oddly low-hanging street lamps casting an eerie yet charming light over the dusty streets.

Juelz adjusted the brim of his hat to shield his eyes from the glare of the lamps. His stomach growled, reminding him he had skipped lunch earlier in favor of a couple more hours' of exploration. That fresh bread smell was more enticing with each step, and he found himself on a path to the General Store. Along with food, he could use some supplies before his evening ride.

In NimblePine, as anyone who had heard of it knew, the unexpected was always just around the corner, but for now, Juelz enjoyed the calm of the evening. His eyes continuously scanned his surroundings, but the townsfolk simply nodded courteously as he passed. It was an expansive, bustling town—a place where the past and present converged seamlessly. Here, amidst the flurry of construction of new brick roads that promised smoother travels and less mud on rainy days, life thrived in vibrant bursts of activity. The streets were lined with an array of businesses, and the air was sweeter than in most other towns he'd ever been in. Taverns, bars, and saloons dotted the landscape, each flowing with energy and music, their doors open to anyone looking for fun and a good drink. The general stores were hubs of activity, carrying goods from lands farther away than most folks would ever travel. Nearby butcher shops displayed cut meats, while dress shops showcased windows filled with the latest fashions, luring in curious passersby. Behind it all,was the steady hammering of iron on iron echoed from the blacksmiths, forging tools, horseshoes and other needs of the town. Somethings overlooked, NimblePine's brothels operated with quiet discretion, catering to the wealthier clientele. Over time Juelz found the local theatre often doubled as a house of pleasure, offering Shakespearean dramas on stage while, in the balconies above, the more well off customers indulged in more intimate performances and services, available only to those with deep pockets and an agreement in secrecy.

As Juelz continued down the road, he marveled once again at all the town had to offer. No matter how many times he visited or how long he stayed, Juelz marveled at the town's curious blend of antiquity and innovation, a place where the familiar warmth of Western charm intertwined with a creeping wave of modernity. Nimblepine was no longer just a frontier town—it had evolved into something far greater, its ambitions visible in every street and structure. The marketplace, once simple, had transformed into a bustling hub of commerce, its stalls stretching as far as the eye could see. Vendors called out their wares, peddling goods from distant lands, while the scent of fresh-baked bread and the aroma of spices and smoke from nearby ovens filled the air.

Beneath the market's familiar chaos, subtle signs of advancement had begun to take root. Libraries, long known for their dusty shelves and timeworn times, now offered strange devices nestled among the books. Resembling tablets of stone yet filled with ever-scrolling texts and vibrant images, these artifacts were powered by unseen mechanisms, mysterious to all but a few. Townsfolk whispered about them, unsure whether to embrace the convenience or fear the magic that seemed to breathe life into the tools.

Even the town's medical facilities had undergone transformation. Where once doctors mixed herbs by hand, now gleamed instruments diagnosed ailments with scary precision. These devices, brought in from The Electric Company, were spoken of in secret tones and settings—some saw them as miracles, others as unsettling. To the common folk, such tools bordered on sorcery, defying their understanding of what a healer should be.

As Juelz continued through the winding streets, he observed more signs of this strange, hybrid existence. The road beneath his feet was mostly cobblestone, yet overhead wires crisscrossed between buildings, carrying unseen energy to street lamps that glowed with an otherworldly light. Nimblepine, in all its contradictions, had become a place where the past and future coexisted uneasily, neither fully yielding to the other.

His gaze landed on a vendor's booth, its display arranged with a meticulousness that stood out even in the busy square. Old-fashioned boots were laid out in perfect rows, each pair bathed in a soft light that seemed to emanate from within the stand itself. It was a calculated display, designed to draw the eye. Only a handful of boots were on show, as if to imply that their scarcity made them more valuable. The glow was subtle but unmistakable— these strange new technologies crept throughout the town. Beside the booth, a young man stood guard, his overalls shimmering faintly in the lamplight. His sharp eyes darted from customer to customer, ready and alert to chase off any would-be thieves or hagglers seeking a deal beneath their station. It was clear that even in a town like Nimblepine, where old and new mingled, the rules of survival had not changed. Money still spoke the loudest. Juelz could feel it in the air, in the tension that thrummed through the streets and behind every transaction. NimblePine was a place where ambition ran high.

"Good day, sir!" the vendor called as Juelz sighed but approached, his tone overly enthusiastic.

"You look like a man who appreciates quality. How about some sturdy boots for yourself? Or, strong man like you surely has a son running around. He needs boots! Only twenty dollars, best deal in town."

Juelz only nodded politely and made a wide path around the booth. "I'm fine," intending to keep moving.

Not one to lose a sale so easily, the vendor called out again. "Fifteen dollars! A steal for such

quality! Come take a look." But one glance was all
Juelz needed to see that this was no ordinary
cobbler. His left eye shone too brightly to be
natural, and his voice carried a little too well over
the heads of the crowd.
He tipped his hat again, "I'm quite all right," and
stepped into the street to get around the stream of
people. Nimblepine's strangeness was a marvel to
observe, but he'd done well so far keeping himself
out of the midst of it.

Juelz squinted at the strange light coming
from one of the streetlamps. Oil lamps, he
understood, but this bulb gave off an unnatural
glow, hanging in its glass box as if lit by magic. He
shook his head and kept walking. Nimblepine had
changed since the last time he'd passed through–
grown in ways he hadn't expected.
As he walked down the busy street, he noticed,
behind the stores, hidden from view, cramped
houses and apartments barely held the families
who struggled to make ends meet. Juelz had once
lived in a place like that, just another body in the
sea of the working people. Now, he had a
different life, though he wasn't sure it was any
easier. He glanced up toward the countryside,
where huge houses and plantations dotted the
landscape. The wealthy lived outside the town,
removed from its grit and noise.
Juelz passed one of the massive warehouses on
his right. He knew these buildings ran the town,

distributing resources and storing the goods that kept Nimblepine alive. Depending on the season, they'd trade or hoard supplies, shaping the town's economy in ways most people didn't think about. He tugged at the brim of his hat, the river breeze carrying the faint sound of a steamboat whistle in the distance. More people. He thought

He scanned the street ahead, taking in the merchants and farmers who had popped up like weeds, filling every empty corner. A small fruit stand caught his attention, a flash of color against the dusty backdrop. Juelz slowed his pace. Staffed by a middle-aged woman with a homely face. Some things never changed, Juelz thought to himself.

This time, he was here for the Dice, but Juelz never had been able to resist detouring through NimblePine. He rarely spent his money here and would rather camp just outside than stay the night, but whenever he needed to get lost in a crowd, or the search for a mark brought him nearby, he always tried to pass through.

Nearing a fruit stand, his stomach rumbled and he began looking out for a moment he might be able to swipe a snack.

He was well practiced in banditry, and he didn't have to wait wrong. As he approached, a man stepped up to the stand and engaged the woman behind it with questions of origin and ripeness. That was just enough diversion for Juelz, with the finesse of an experienced thief, used the advantage of the crowd to, swift as the wind, snatch a peach from the edge of the table and slip it into his coat pocket. It was nothing compared to the banks and houses he was used to, but the warmup gave him some satisfaction.

The sound of metal on metal filled the air. His attention was caught by a three-wheeled cart rumbling down the road, prompting anyone walking in its path to scramble to the side. Juelz had heard of these before, but had not seen one. This cart was powered by its own internal mechanism and made a mighty din clanking down the street. He decided to duck into a saloon and rush up to the upper balconies to watch it go by.

Even before it reached him, the odors it emitted washed away the smell of bread and instead filled the air with the scents of soot and overheating metal. Craning over the balcony railing, he peered into a hole in the cart's siding. The operator, noticing Juelz's curious gaze, gave him a bored look and went back to piloting the strange cart. Juelz scoffed and stepped back to lean against a nearby beam. Surely, with such strange inventions, they would be more used to gawkers. The cart continued clanging and banging its way down the newly laid brown brick road, leaving a trail of black smoke in its wake. The smell was unbearable. As the smoke washed over him, he and the other patrons of the saloon all began to cough, leaving him both fascinated and repelled.

Once he got ahold of himself again, Juelz watched the crowd's reaction. The townsfolk parted like a sea before it, creating a clear path for the wheeled wonder, but no one stopped to stare or point. He couldn't help but grimace.

Despite the marvel of self-propelled machines, he had already decided that nothing could replace the reliability and grace of Santana, his trusty horse. To him, nothing could match the power of galloping down the road trailing dust, not in a smoke-belching cart. He smoothed his coat aside to retrieve the peach he had pocketed earlier. He took a hearty bite, the crisp sound of the fruit's flesh breaking under his teeth filling his ears.

Returning to ground floor, he remembered his goal and set back off down the street. "I'll trade you a fat pig!" vendors continued to call to each other. Juelz couldn't help but smile to himself at such ordinary haggling amidst the town's modern marvels. He returned to scanning the street, looking for any indication of a general store. Passing yet another bar, Juelz finished the last bites of the peach, the sweetness lingered on his tongue. a distraction from his real purpose. He wasn't here to sightsee. He needed a new blanket and a satchel that didn't have holes big enough to lose half his things. His gaze sharpened as he finally spotted the general store tucked around a corner.

He stepped inside, the scent of wood and leather hit him as the door creaked shut. But before he could take more than a few steps, a familiar voice cut through the air, stopping him cold.

"Should've seen the look on his face when we busted in on him on the pot—priceless," the voice said, followed by a laugh that seemed to lumber out.

Juelz's stomach dropped. He'd recognize that smug drawl anywhere.

"You gotta be shittin' me," he muttered under his breath, disbelief tightening his jaw. His heart thudded hard, as he looped around a shelf, moving with care to avoid being seen. Without a second thought, he slipped back onto the street, blending back into the bustling crowd before anyone noticed.

Instinctively, he strode back the way he had come and slid into the bar he'd just passed, choosing a seat close enough to the window to see out, but not so obvious that any passer could see and recognize him.

Through the dirt-fogged window, a group of figures came into view in the same direction he had just come. He counted five men, all but one in long navy blue coats. The fifth wore distinct gray, and they all stood out from the rest of the townsfolk.

Welp, time's up, time to go, Juelz concluded to himself, knowing his supplies would have to wait. He couldn't afford a confrontation today. Whatever the five men were discussing, giving occasional nods or glances around, he was too far to read any of their lips, and certainly couldn't hear them over the low din of the bar. The presence of Pinkertons in NimblePine was no small matter and could have disastrous consequences for the coming night's ride.

A sixth figure came into view, a notable figure due to his sheer size and a coat of dark red fur, but he weaved expertly through the stream of people to the group of men. They had drifted closer to the open door, and his voice was loud enough to reach Juelz even muffled by the window.

"The rest were here… well, we're pretty close to… Just took three days, only a matter of…" Juelz realized the man in the red coat was Mayor Hodges, which boded even worse for Juelz. Pinkertons stalking the streets meant he couldn't waltz around recklessly. The group continued to drift toward the front door of the bar, and Juelz' mind whirled with thoughts of escape. He couldn't afford to be caught, not now, not when he was so close to such an important score.

He glanced around the dimly-lit room, his eyes finally settling on a back door near the corner, propped open slightly. Casually, as if he were any other patron, he stood up and sauntered toward the back, and just as he slipped out he heard the mayor's laughter enter the front door behind him.

The night had begun to cool down, and a breeze brushed against his face and he stepped into a deserted alleyway. He closed the door completely behind him, cutting off the sounds of the barroom. Then, he allowed himself a moment to collect himself, pulling his hat low over his face before setting off again.

He could only guess why the Pinkertons might be in NimblePine, and with the mayor no less. In all his visits to the town, he couldn't recall ever seeing them around. It could always be a coincidence, but Juelz didn't believe in that sort of thing. Even if it had nothing to do with the coming job, something big must have been brewing in NimblePine.

A ways down the street, away from the bar and general store, he cut back into the dwindling crowd of the main road. By this time, people were beginning to head home for supper, and the vendors were closing down.

"Cakes all sold. Come back tomorrow!" cried one, and he was met with disappointed grumbles before the line for his stand dissipated.

Juelz checked is pocketwatch, realizing time was slipping past him. It wouldn't do to be late, or be left out on the street without other people to hide him. As he made his way back to the train station, he passed a heated argument along the side of the road.

"I'm not a beggar, this is the World, and we're trapped here," a man shouted, his voice seasoned with desperation and anger.
Nearby, a group of men stood at the edge of the street, their voices rising in heated debate.
"I'm tellin' you, it's the mayor's fault! Taxes keep goin' up while we get nothin' in return," one man barked, his face flushed with frustration.
"Taxes? Ha! It's those damn factories. Every year they cut wages and expect us to work longer," another shot back, crossing his arms defiantly. "They don't care about us. Just their pockets."
A third voice jumped in, rough and tired. "You're both wrong. It's the damn railroad comin' through. They don't care how it affects the farms. They want land and don't care what they destroy to get it."
The argument echoed back and forth, others in the crowd chiming in as more bystanders gathered, taking sides. Some argued agreement about the mayor's corruption, while others complained about the factory bosses or the railroad's greed. Each opinion clashed loudly with the next, embodying NimblePine's split nature—everyone was angry, but no one could agree on who to blame.
This was NimblePine. A place where voices collided like hammer on anvil, and arguments

bled from the saloons into the streets, echoing late into the night. It was a town divided by every issue under the sun and moon, where every man had something to say, and no one wanted to listen.

NimblePine, Juelz realized, was a town split in two. Some, like him, saw it as a sanctuary—a place of opportunity. But for others, it was nothing more than a prison, where they were forced to scrape by, trapped in a town that was slowly succumbing to sickness.

Everywhere he looked, there were signs of it. People coughing in the streets, children with pale faces, a man hunched over at the corner. The Doctor always had a line outside its door, folks waiting for whatever small remedies were available.

The poor, crammed into tight, unsanitary quarters, blamed the wealthy for keeping the best medicines and doctors for themselves. Juelz had overheard it all. "They sit in their fine homes with the good stuff, while we get the scraps," one woman had spat, her voice ragged from sickness. The wealthy, in turn, resented the poor for bringing illness into their world. "They bring disease with them," he'd heard someone murmur in a tavern, the man's nose wrinkled in disgust. "If they weren't packed in like rats, we wouldn't have these outbreaks."

This was the true heart of NimblePine—a town at war with itself, both sides trapped in a cycle of blame and fear, like a shadow hanging over everything,

The distant whistle of the train sliced through the evening air, snapping Juelz out of his thoughts. He turned and hurried toward the station. The railroad illuminated the town, casting long shadows that stretched over NimblePine in fingers of light. Juelz watched as the train ascended the iron ramp, a marvel of engineering that elevated it to the second level of the central station. The three-story structure loomed above the town. It was more than just a station— it was a hub where old-world dust met the gleaming steel of new and modern. The train, with its lights glowing beneath the wheels and along its sleek front, cut through the haze of dusk, washing the streets in its glow.

The rhythmic clanking of the train's wheels grew louder, accompanied by the groan of metal as it came to a stop at the platform. He felt for the worn paper of the ticket in his pocket. The rhythmic clanking of the train's wheels on its tracks grew louder, and the train groaned as it came to rest at the platform. As he approached the conductor at the platform's entrance, Juelz pulled the ticket from his pocket, handing it over with a nod. The conductor gave it a quick glance before waving him through. Juelz took one last look at the town behind him, then stepped onto the train, the hiss of steam rising as he stepped onto The Rolling Dice.

Sam
1861

The wagon tilted violently, the dry, uneven Texas terrain made the ride anything but easy. Outside, the steady rhythm of hoofbeats echoed in the oppressive heat, accompanied by the murmurs of the guards. Sam could hear them speaking in low voices, sometimes a chuckle, though what they spoke about in their conversations remained a mystery, muffled by the creak of the wagon and the jangling of chains.

Amidst the rattles and groans of wood, Lewis kept on with his half-baked ideas. "Now, hear me out, right? What you do is, you take a train, see–" Sam inhaled deeply beside him, trying to stretch his ribs as much as his shackles would allow. His thoughts were distant, disconnected from the scene around him, though he could feel Lewis' shoulder pressing into his.

"Hey, uh, you okay?" Lewis nudged him. Sam didn't answer, his mind already wandering toward darker thoughts.

Sam listened to only every other word, dismissing Lewis' schemes as idle talk. He wasn't buying into it, but it was something to distract him from the relentless creak of the cart. Outside, the guards had fallen silent, though the snap of reins could occasionally be heard.

"So, you take the train," Lewis pressed on. His voice was hushed, almost conspiratorial.

"Uh huh," Sam answered flatly, deciding the sounds of the road weren't so bad after all.

"And then you hit a casino."

The thought was absurd. The guards' laughter flared up again from the front of the wagon, one of them calling something over his shoulder that Sam didn't quite catch. But their voices, filled with easy authority, carried a weight that brought Sam back to reality. There was no escape, no casino waiting. Only more chains.

Three weeks prior, under the cover of a new moon, Sam and two others had made a desperate bid for freedom. That same night, as they fled, Sam had witnessed red streaks of fire cutting across the sky. He'd taken it as a sign, an omen of something bigger, something hopeful.

Their freedom was short-lived. After three grueling days and less than five miles, the barking of hounds and approach of the milk men signaled their impending recapture. His companions had slowed him down, maybe clumsy and weak from days without rest or food. One had twisted an ankle on loose rocks, forcing Sam and the other man to half-carry him. That was their undoing. When they were overtaken, Sam barely resisted. He couldn't. He should've left his companions.bThe exhaustion, both mental and physical, had left him hollow.

Now, shackled once more, Sam sat in the overcrowded wagon, packed shoulder-to-shoulder with nine other men. Designed to hold eight, the wagon felt claustrophobic. Shackles bolted to the walls held most of them, while one was chained cross-legged to the floor. Among the others was Lewis, a gaunt young man in his early twenties, wearing a threadbare t-shirt filled with holes. A tenth man, more defiant than the rest, was tied by the wrists and forced to walk alongside the wagon, but when they'd first set out and the snap of reins pushed them forward, even his spirit seemed to break. Not Lewis', though.

"You take the cabins first," Lewis continued, leaning closer to Sam. His voice was barely a whisper, wary of the guards overhearing.

Sheer foolishness, Sam thought. Though Lewis was a shining light through the despair, his whispers got annoying. "And then the games, you know, that the white folks play, with the cards and all that. Foolishness, Sam thought. How could they, men not even permitted the basic right to read, hope to get a train.

Sam attempted to focus on anything else: a bug crawling across the wagon floor, the groaning creak of aged wood beneath them. Anything but Lewis' ..ideas, which were starting to wear on him. The others were mostly silent, some brooding, some staring blankly at the planks of the walls. Sam recognized those looks and often wore them himself. It was the same one that appeared when someone witnessed unbearable cruelty, a way of retreating deep within oneself.

"Look," Lewis said, undeterred by Sam's lack of response. "I know you don't believe me, but there's plenty of us in those card rooms. I've seen it." He gestured with his hands, careful not to clink his chains.

Sam's silence deepened, letting his weary, drawn face speak for him. Again, Lewis was caught up in his own thoughts and kept on without slowing.

"Yeah, all of us using what we got, you know? Like everything they use us for." He turned slightly to look Sam directly in the face, "And then we get respect, and maybe, just maybe, we turn this thing into something real. Like freedom." Then, he finally quieted, and his eyes drifted up to the bits of sky peeking through the canvas.

Lewis stayed quiet once they'd righted themselves. A small mercy, Sam thought, and they all stayed quiet until suddenly, the wagon shook violently, tossing the men against one another.

Sam clenched as he struggled to maintain his balance. His body ached, and wanted rest. I just want to sleep, he thought wearily.

Outside, one of the overseers barked an order to the group, pulling his horse around to circle the wagon. Sam glanced up briefly, catching a glimpse of the man's leather vest, dusted from the road. His movements were practiced, almost lazy, as though their captivity was routine. Maybe it was.

"Alright, boys, it's on foot from here," the overseer called out from behind the wagon. The wagon came to a slow stop, kicking up dust around them.

Sam's stomach sank. The prisoners shuffled out one by one, their legs stiff from hours of confinement. The guards had already dismounted, standing in a loose group, rifles slung casually over their shoulders.

The men were counted, then shackled in a line, each man connected to the next by heavy chains. Sam's legs almost protested as they were forced to walk but he talked to them out of it. The wagon was likely too heavy for the terrain ahead. Or maybe they just wanted to make them suffer more, but Sam knew better than to ask. The heat pressed down on them, unrelenting.

Hours passed, it felt all too familiar, a single-file line, each man shackled to the next. They marched on, their chains clanking with every step. As the day turned to night an back to day, the relentless march continued under the beating sun. By midday the next day, the sun blazed overhead with no clouds to break its unforgiving hat. To distract himself, Sam scanned his surroundings for any details that might hint at their location.

 Over the years, the once lush landscape had thinned, leaving only the occasional tree to shade them and long stretches of open grassland. As Sam chewed their dry, tasteless food, Sam's mind wandered back to the moment of their capture, it was the hounds, the moment the hounds had caught their scent, the sudden, heart-stopping realization that they were not going to make it. He remembered the fight that ensued, the struggle, and the overwhelming force that had dragged them back into chains.

He felt the urge to run, to fight, but the days since then had taught him the reality of their situation. He remembered the red snake of light streaking across the sky on the night of their escape. He had taken it as an omen of hope, but now he wasn't so sure.

 He glanced up at the sky now, remembering that red streak, that strange moment of hope. It seemed so distant now, like a dream he could barely recall.

If any man stumbled, the guards' hands would twitch toward their weapons, though none made a move. The day wore on, the chains clinking with every step, the sun bearing down without mercy.

"Keep moving," a guard ordered, his voice sharp.Riding alongside and sometimes ahead, the overseers kept a close watch. Though few in number, the weapons slung across their backs and waists leant them plenty of advantage. If they made a break for it now, they couldn't even rely on the trees to shield them. Seeing him look around, one of the overseers guided his horse to block Sam's view. "Please boy, make my day. Go on, run for it, you could probably make it. I won't say anything." Sam, knowing the bait for what it was, only shook his head and averted his eyes. Ahead, the faint outlines of a town began to take shape on the horizon. Smoke curled lazily into the air from a fire pit. The guards exchanged knowing glances, anticipation of rest and food lightening their mood. For the prisoners, however, the sight of the town stirred only apprehension.

Once night fell after the second day, Sam found himself again chained next to Lewis, who leaned in close while they were settling down to sleep. He leaned over until his chin was just over Sam's shoulder.

"Psst, hey," Lewis whispered again, undeterred by Sam's silence. "I've been thinking about the name."

"Are you serious?" Simmering in sudden frustration, Sam leaned away. Lewis continued anyway, as always.

"I thought more about it. I was thinking—"

"Are you trying to lose a hand?" Lewis rolled his eyes and fell back to his spot.

Gradually, as they continued their march the next day, a different aroma began to fill the air, cutting through the stench of sweat and dust. The unmistakable scent of cooking food. Sam's stomach growled, a pang of hunger stabbing through him. As they drew nearer, the scent grew stronger, richer, mingling with the smoky tang that drifted on the breeze. Sam lifted his head, straining to see the source of the aroma.

Ahead, smoke curled into the sky in lazy tendrils, rising from a cluster of buildings that marked the edge of a town. The sight of it stirred apprehension in Sam. Towns meant people, and people meant danger, but also the possibility of better food. As they approached, Sam saw a figure stoking a fire, the flames dancing and flickering in the late afternoon light. Behind him stood a looming black building. His mind raced with possibilities.

"Psst, hey," Lewis broke through his thoughts, "I got it, we could call it." Sam physically shook Lewis off this time, shoving him away as best he could with shackled hands, earning them both a bark from an overseer and a shove back in line. Lewis' face fell, but he kept his gaze on Sam and leaned back in, quick as anything, as soon as the overseers were distracted again.

"The Rolling Dice, we'd call it," while Sam stared stoically ahead.

Oliver.

Orbiting Earth.

The wail of emergency klaxons filled the air, their relentless screech ricocheting through the confines of the spaceship. The corridors were bathed in a harsh red glow, casting ominous shadows as the crew navigated the tight confines with urgency. Alarms echoed from all directions– above, below, and even from concealed compartments in the walls Oliver had never seen. Amidst the chaos, the crew members scrambled toward safety, frenetic and desperate. Mia was the first to burst into the safe room, her expression a mixture of worry and panic, eyes wide. Close behind her, Alison stumbled in, groggy and disoriented, struggling to shake off the deep sleep she had been pulled from so abruptly. She had always been the heaviest sleeper among them.

Eva took up a post by the door to usher each of them in. The hidden entrance had been part of their safety drills, a place meant to offer sanctuary in the event of an emergency, but the reality of its use knocked the drills from their head, so more than one of them almost missed the turn.

Olive sunk to the floor, his back pressed against the cold metal wall, forearms resting on his knees as he tried to steady his breathing. He had been through countless drills, but knowing this alarm was real made all the difference in the world. Each blare of the klaxon seemed to shake his very bones.

Von took a lower bunk by Oliver's shoulder, his back against the same wall, watching the unfolding scene with a sober, almost detached expression. The emergency lights reflected off his glasses, creating an eerie glint that made everything feel so much worse. They were safe for the moment, and had not passed any intruders or damage on their way here, but uncertainty hung heavy in the air.

"Something is very wrong, Oliver," Kendall announced as she joined him on the floor. She had to scream between alarm blares.

"No shit." Oliver didn't even try to yell, and instead contorted his face into the most unimpressed, sarcastic expression he could muster and hoped she could read lips.

The last of the crew filtered into the room, and Eva slid the door shut behind them, muffling the alarms. She and Captain Moody would clear the ship and retrieve them once all was clear.

Hopefully, all they would find was a faulty sensor, and everyone would be allowed to go back to bed.

Kendall practically vibrated next to him, both knees bouncing in anxiety.

"Relax," he said in a voice he hoped was reassuring. "We've been moving continuously until just now. If there was an intruder, they would've been caught light years back during the station inspection."

All eyes turned to Von, seeking the input of the oldest crew member in the room.

Von pressed his thumbs to his temples and shrugged, "Hell, I don't know," and all their eyes fell away again except Oliver, who waited to catch Von's eye.

"You good?" Von gave a half-hearted thumbs-up.

"Seriously, though, does anyone know what's going on? Like, anything?" Alison spoke up, audibly restraining her own panic. "Okay, what station did we leave last?"

"Delilah, probably," Oliver shrugged, "I never bother to check. Who really pays attention to the fueling stops? I was asleep last refueling anyway." He gestured to Kendall, who shook her head. "Yeah, me too."

"Where is that damn ape? If he can't get to the safe room—"

"Junon" came Terry's voice from a high shelf, where he had been quietly perched, his presence forgotten.

Of course he knew. Terry's memory and intelligence were unnerving at times. Possessing a 143 IQ, he was the smartest being on the ship, and wasn't one for socializing, so he had an eerie aura around him.

"Oh, don't worry. This," he raised four fingers in air-quotes, "'ship' wasn't my first choice either. My project was approved, and due to budgetary hurdles I was thrown onto the first ship available." He gestured vaguely to the ship around him.

The room fell quiet except for the muffled blaring of continued alarms.

"Perhaps it's bad luck for primates to fly." Terry gave a forced chuckle, and Oliver gave a sour laugh in response.

Just then, the sound of rapid footsteps echoed outside, growing louder and more urgent. Everyone held their breath. The footsteps stopped abruptly right on the other side of the door, and Kendall got carefully up to check the lock.

As her hand contacted the handle, the door burst open, and Eva stormed in. Her eyes scanned the room, quickly counting heads. At 26, Eva was formidable not only for a pilot, but also for her age. She was still dressed, as always, in her standard gray uniform that seemed almost like a second skin. Her gun was drawn, not unusual, given the circumstances, but the blood dripping down her forearm drew a hushed gasp from the room.

"Finally, some answers," Mia exclaimed, "What's happening? The computers again?"

"Where's Moody?" Oliver asked, hoping for some leadership.

"I'm glad you're all safe," Eva exhaled. Her tone suggested relief, but her face remained tense. "Come with me."
Oliver rose to his feet, joints popping from sitting with his knees up. It became clear, as they fell into line behind Eva, that whatever was wrong, they were about to find out.

He tried again, "What happened? What failed—"
Eva took off, and his words were lost behind him in a rush of lightheadedness.

"What—" Several voices started as a soft tremble shuddered through the ship.

At that moment, the artificial gravity failed, sending a lurching wave of panic through the group. Oliver was thrown forward and up, his head striking a pipe running along the ceiling with a sharp crack. Pain flared, blinding and intense. Around him, the other crew members were thrown against the walls and ceiling. Only Eva and Terry were able to recover fast enough to catch themselves against a doorway and a water pipe. Eva also caught Mia despite her own disarray and guided her to a handhold.

"This way, folks, just ahead!" Eva said

Struggling to re-orient himself with the sudden weightlessness, Oliver managed to grasp another pipe and point himself in the direction Eva was headed. He touched the top of his head to check for injury and grimaced, but no blood. Looking around, he checked to make sure the rest of the crew was still following Eva and narrowly saved Von from drifting off into the center of the hall.

Once they were all through the doorway Eva had first grabbed onto, she swiftly input her code and initiated the manual close and airlock. They all watched anxiously as the door seemed to take an eternity to seal.

"This is crazy," he muttered to himself, finding relief in the hiss of the door sealing shut, trying not to think about what would happen if something went wrong on this side of the door rather than the other.

As they hurried along, Eva turned and Oliver realized that the alarms hadn't rung since she burst into the safe room. "Listen up! Think! Did any of you see anything off or out of place?"

No response. They were all focused on propelling down the hallway without stranding themselves in open air. Oliver shook his head. Everything had been perfectly normal for weeks.

Eva glanced at her wrist communicator with a grave expression.

"I can't afford to wait to debrief you. I'm so sorry, Captain Moody is dead. I found her after I got all of you in the safe room." Murmuring immediately filled the corridor. Oliver felt as if he'd been hit by a wave of cold water.

"What happened?" Kendall's voice rose above the others.

Eva's eyes darted into each room they passed, and she took the time to close and seal any open doorways. "I'm not sure," she admitted, her voice thick and trembling. She glanced at her wrist again, "Oxygen levels are dropping. Not quickly, but still. We'll want to keep moving."

"I was monitoring the cameras and saw her heading to her room to rest, like all of you."

Oliver gave a strong push and propelled himself up beside her. "That means there really is someone out there, right?" He tried to keep his voice low.

"All areas of the ship have been cleared," Eva responded without faltering.

The thought chilled him. There was no place to hide on the Dawn, yet somewhere, someone had used an unaccounted-for access card. They were approaching Captain Moody's quarters, and Eva spoke up again.

"I know you all are—I know you've seen some things, but I don't know if this is something you want in your memory bank."

Despite the warning, curiosity got the better of him as they passed the captain's room. The sight that greeted him turned his stomach. From his vantage near the ceiling, he could see Captain Moody clearly on her stomach on the bed, legs pointed toward the door and half under the covers, head twisted, her eyes staring down her own back.

"This can't be happening."

He glanced back at the rest of the crew. Alison and Mia quickened deliberately avoided looking inside and scrambled to pass faster. Von let out a low, "Oh, man," as he passed trailing behind them. A couple of doors down, Eva finally beckoned them to a stop outside the security room.

"Waste disposal kits, water, carbohydrates, and vitamin supplements. We all have to leave immediately." She pointed at one or two people as she said each, assigning them to gather enough for everyone. Her voice was back to the strong, commanding tone they were used to, and it helped Oliver to fall back into the familiar routine of following orders.

"Get going," she said, and they all shot off toward their assigned supply location.

They had practiced this countless times. Regroup at the security office. Emergency water down the right hallway. Food and supplements the next door down. Emergency field kits the opposite direction. However, like most of what they had experienced since being rudely awakened, the reality didn't come so naturally. Each person focused on their immediate tasks, the importance of every second not lost on them as tiredness began to set in and Eva's communicator beeped to remind them of the ship's failing systems. Oliver gathered emergency kits with Terry and hurried back to the security door. Alison, more awake now, moved with practiced efficiency, gathering the most necessary data drives while Mia shoved carbohydrate and vitamin supplements into a bag. Von, usually so composed, fumbled in the lack of gravity.

Oliver rejoined Eva across the hall from the security office, where she was rapidly checking the escape pods, opening the doors, and getting them ready for launch. Suddenly, her course shifted and she slipped into the security room, where the mission records and emergency logs were kept, and Oliver realized that none of them knew her very well. He stuck his head into the security room.

Eva was already busy at the terminal, muttering to herself. "Checked what was logged in cargo…saw nothing…Why didn't I think…that first?" Her fingers flew across the keyboard. "There it is! Okay, then…" The screen turned green and began to blink. The tapped at the keyboard, but it gave no response. She moved swiftly to another terminal and tried again, but this screen also began to blink. "What…attack is this?" Oliver heard all the others returning to the escape pods behind him.

"What's wrong?" He called after the movement stopped, trying to keep his voice low.

Eva was now taking an access panel off the wall to rummage in the wires. "The security system, it's locked up."

"Ah, there," she said after some more rummaging, and both terminals went black.

A shiver ran through Oliver. "It's cold. We should get to the pods." Eva didn't look at him, continuing to wrestle one of the terminals back to life.

"Cold?"

"Yeah, it was kind of like–" He trailed off as a soft whistling sound caught his attention. Then the ship gave another violent shudder, and the emergency blast door closed across the corridor they had come through, cutting off the rest of the ship. Then the whistling sound was gone.

"This should only take another second. We need to know what's wrong." Now she looked back at him. "You said cold?"

He nodded, "For a second there." With the other life support systems failing, the heaters were surely starting to fall behind by now, but Eva's brow furrowed, and she left the terminal to glance out into the hall.

"Go make sure the others are ready to go and get in your pod. Don't wait up–I'll be right behind you."

"Don't take too long." Reluctantly, Oliver crossed the hall and found that the others had distributed the supplies between all of the pods and were almost ready to go. Terry, Mia, and Alison were secured and enclosed. Kendall and Von were in their pods but seemed to be waiting for him.

"Where's Eva?" Kendall started, and the ship gave its most violent lurch yet, dislodging Oliver from the wall he was using to propel himself across the room and sending him hurtling into the side of his open pod, hitting his head on the door hinge. There was a series of pops and clicks from the corridor, like distorting metal, and the sucking sound of a failing seal. Eva appeared, shouting, at the edge of his vision, a blur of distorted shapes. It sounded as if her voice was coming through deep water, and his head throbbed. He reached out for any handhold on the pod's surface to pull himself in, but didn't have the strength through his own heartbeat pounding in his head.

Eva's shouting came closer until it was just behind him, and he felt her helping him into the pod and pulling the harness around him.

"Can you hear me?" A continuous shiver was traveling up and down the ship now, and Oliver could see Eva struggling to hold on. He tried to respond, but only managed a garbled mumble, his head and right shoulder pinging off the pod wall as he fought to stay conscious and help her strap him in.

"You took a hard hit. You're safe now." Even though he could barely understand, the conviction in her voice was comforting, and he was able to hold on long enough to hear the pod's door hydraulics kick in.

Lewis
1861

Lewis' body ached from the relentless march under the scorching sun, and his mind was constantly on edge. The town they had arrived in was odd, unsettling in a way he couldn't immediately place. The air was thick with a harsh, metallic scent, like rusted steel and iron, mingling with something even fouler beneath it. The unnatural odor clawed at his senses as it filled his nose and mouth with each breath.

As they were herded toward the auction block, Lewis couldn't help but notice the way the townspeople watched, their eyes cold and calculating. Sweat trickled down his back as his eyes scanned the crowd, noting the crowd that had come to inspect the goods.

Under the grey sky, the crack of a whip sliced through the air.

"Two hundred!" bellowed the auctioneer in his weathered brown hat.

"Ladies and gentlemen, we have a fine selection of able-bodied workers here. Consider this one.

He can cook, clean, and is exceptionally strong."
He gestured to a man ahead of Lewis in line.

The spectacle unfolded on a temporary wooden platform in the town square. They stood in line, each positioned so that potential buyers could better examine them.

"Two-hundred five!" the auctioneer shouted, gesturing to a man in the crowd with his hand up.

Something in the town itself smelled. The metallic smell lingered in the air, this time mixed with the faint sourness to it. Lewis couldn't understand how free people could bear to live in a place like this—a place where all the air was thick and everything seemed tainted, it was like rust settling over the very soil.

He was grateful that it was an overcast day, at least, and the clouds shaded them from the worst of the heat.

"We got 215, can I get 220?"

"One escape on record, but he's been reformed," The auctioneer gave a barely noticeable pause, giving the man a sharp glance. "He'll amaze you with his work ethic!"

"Once his feet heal, invite folks over, have dinner, have him dance in your living room, perfect for company."

"225!" A very large man in the crowd called out his bid.

"230," another voice countered.

"Going once, twice, sold!" the auctioneer called, and the man was led off the platform.

As the auction continued, that peculiar smell wafted back into the air and fell over the square. Bidders raised their hands to bid, the auctioneer called numbers and sometimes declared "Sold!" before the respective slave was briskly removed from the platform and delivered to the winning bidder in a ritual that repeated throughout the day.

Lewis scanned the crowd, his eyes flicking nervously between the crowd's faces. He tried to avoid locking eyes with anyone in particular, fearing the cold, calculating gazes that appraised him like livestock. He could feel the weight of each stare. The scrutiny was almost unbearable, and Lewis felt cold sweat trickle down his back.

Among the onlookers, a very large man dressed in all black stood out, towering over his peers and showing no sign of being affected by the heat.

"We'll start the bidding for this strong man here. Look at those muscles! A hard worker, indeed!" The men before Lewis were sold for all manner of prices from $175 to $600, but the prices themselves didn't mean anything to Lewis. They were all still trapped in a cycle, and the only hope he had was the slim chance that his new owner might be a shade less cruel than the last.

The sun had begun to go down behind Mount Ulrich, and there were only five men left behind

Lewis, all of them grateful for the diminishing sunlight. The auction was loud, a constant din punctuated by shoes and occasional disputes among the bidders. Some people merely raised their hands, while others shouted their bids and fanned themselves vigorously.

"We'll start this one at 300." Lewis clenched his jaw as the auctioneer gestured to him.

"320!" a voice from the crowd countered quickly.

Born on a southern plantation, Lewis typically worked in kitchens and gardens, but did occasional field work. He had a quick wit but surprisingly absent-minded tendencies. His mother was a nurturing woman, and she often marveled at her son's ability to grasp complex ideas effortlessly while simultaneously tripping over his own feet or forgetting where he put his toys.

The crowd had diminished throughout the day, so the auctioneer called to gather the few stragglers left, "Come, come!" he bellowed, "A prime boy! Got a female back home?" He bent toward the front row and lowered his voice conspiratorially, "Breed 'em, and trade god's gifts, the little heathens," he paused dramatically, "to us!"

A scattered laugh went through the crowd. The auctioneer, quick to capitalize on good humor, zeroed in on one person near the front.

"You look like a dashing fellow. I'm sure you have a house, yes?"

He received a nod and added, "And in that house, I'm sure you have company. You need entertainment!"

"350!" Shouted a bearded man from the first few rows.

"375," a woman countered.

"Closer, closer, folks," the auctioneer urged.

"400!" The strange man in black barely had to raise his voice to be heard. His bid cast a brief silence over the square, but another man shortly called another bid, and another, and another, but the man eventually called out a bid for $500 and another silence fell. This time, it stuck, and no one raised their voices or hands to bid against him. The bidder in the front grimaced, tapped his foot pensively, and disappeared down the street with a frown. As the fat man's bid was settled, Lewis felt a chill. Something about the man sent a silent warning that made Lewis' skin prickle with unease.

"Sold," declared the auctioneer, "to the gentleman in the back!"

Just like the others, Lewis was led off of the platform and approached by a burly man who must have worked for the man in black. Payment was settled, and Lewis was clasped in loose chains around his waist and wrists and yanked through the crowd, stumbling and almost falling as they got closer to the man in black.

Lewis' heart sank. Each step closer deepened his dread. His instincts screamed for him to turn and run, but he was frozen, ensnared in those empty eyes.

The man's eyes were dark pits, absorbing everything around him and giving nothing back. What kind of fate awaited him now? Between the layers of fine clothing, there was an air of something dark, something Lewis couldn't quite put his finger on. It was something that made the hair on the back of Lewis's neck stand up. It wasn't just the rich fabric or the man's stiff formal stance. It was as if he wore a shadow, not only that but the man had won the screaming contest, being quiet.

Eventually, they reached a pair of wagons, one without horses, and the man turned and fixed him with a smile that didn't reach his eyes.

"Good afternoon. Welcome." His voice was smooth, almost kind, but so deep it send shivers down Lewis' spine. He placed pudgy hands together, "My name is Sylvester Hodges. Please, this way." He looked at the man holding Lewis' chains and gestured to the horseless carriage with his eyes, which they all gathered around.
The politeness was unnerving, as if the man in black were inviting a guest rather than taking possession of a slave. Lewis wondered to himself

where they could be headed, where such strange
behavior could come from.

"How are you, my boy? Are you well?" his new
master called from opposite him, settling
comfortably into his seat. His tone had a facade
of sincerity that, like his smile, didn't spread to
any other area of his face.

"Yeeess, we'll take good care of you all."

"All?" Lewis echoed in a small, nervous voice.

At that, Sylvester only raised his eyebrows
suggestively. Back at the auction, they could still
hear the auctioneer calling bids, and then there
was a booming reaction from the remaining
crowd. Lewis resisted the urge to turn and stare,
reminding himself that he had a new fate to worry
about. Instead, he allowed his eyes to scan
Sylvester's face as discreetly as he could.

He obviously had some sort of power in this
part of the world, or everyone was afraid of him.
He didn't seem completely evil. He certainly had a
lot of money, and maybe Lewis' high price meant
he wouldn't have such a bad time. As Lewis
wrestled with his thoughts, a familiar but
unsettling sound reached his ears. He recognized
it instantly, when was finally able to focus.

The chain gang–larger than usual, judging by the
volume as it got closer. Sylvester leaned out the
still-open door to greet his new acquisitions.
Lewis tried to count them, but they crowded
together in rows, and he lost count. His heart

sank as he realized: this was every man at the auction. Half the crowd must have been bidding for Sylvester, who opened his arms in welcome as the shuffling died down.

"Welcome!" he boomed. "Come, come, you poor devils, we'll be taking good care of you now." Lewis was brought to join the group, and they all stood shuffling from foot to foot.

"Congratulations to all! You are now the property of the Hodges'." The faces around him mirrored Lewis' own. Clearly, none of them had heard of the Hodges' until this man, which was strange, since they apparently had the money and men to buy up the entire day's auction. Scanning the faces of the others, he eventually noticed Sam, standing on the opposite edge of the gang with a face like stone. That eased some of Lewis' worry, but it was like a trickle of water over a wildfire. He tried to lean into Sam's line of sight, but Sam either ignored or didn't see him.

"You should count yourself fortunate." Sylvester smiled lazily. "We are a land of peace and privacy. We shall cherish you all!" and with that, the smile vanished, and he abruptly turned his back while the overseers went about organizing the chain gang and herding them into the horse-drawn wagon.

Despite the strangeness and promise of peace, being loaded into the wagon was no different than any other. Stragglers were shoved and cuffed over the head. One man was bodily shoved into the back of the wagon because they were so tightly packed that he couldn't climb in. Then, there was a final headcount and the overseers climbed into the front of the wagon, shook the reins, and they were off.

They drove until the only light in the sky was red and orange. Once out of the town and the public eye, some of the men began to weep, and their sobs mixed with the creak of the wheels and floor. Lewis and Sam sat on the floor, their knees pressed to their chests, next to each other once again. Lewis had so many questions, but he knew better than to ask them now. Who could these Hodges' be, and where were they being taken? Everything so far had been so strange and unpredictable, from the way Sylvester Hodges had spoken to them all, to the horseless wagon that he had climbed into. As the carriage rocked with dips in the road, Lewis let his mind wander to all the possibilities the future held and fought to stave off the tiredness of the day.

Corey
1872

Alex and Tony maintained their stance at their post while Corey pressed against the sliding door at the right end of the car, easing it open. Two hours had passed since his last patrol, and it was time once again to traverse the compartments of the Rolling Dice according to protocol.

As soon as he passed into the first cabin, the train came alive with activity, illuminated by flickering candles and the sporadic electric light bulb. The Dice was as crowded as Corey had ever seen it. He inhaled deeply, unclipping the nightstick at his hip so it was easily accessible, and began his walk. The cabins were carefully designed, but servers still had to slide carefully between tables. Nearly every seat was occupied, with men and women intertwined and warm with booze. Their laughter mingled with the clinking of glass and murmur of conversation, dealers calling and shuffling, players yelling stories over one-another to be heard.

He passed a woman dancing atop a table to his right, her head tilted and shoulders hunched to avoid bumping against the ceiling, her movements drawing cheers from onlookers. To his left, a man serenaded a lady in a green with a drunken ramble, his voice far too loud for how close he leaned to her ear. The crowd was rowdy, for sure, but so far no one had gotten out of hand.

Maybe it would be a good night. Usually, he had to be on high-alert to break up card-table spats, or even the occasional all-out brawl. The train drew all kinds: tradesmen, lawmen, outlaws. All packed together as thickly as honey in a jar, and such close quarters were bound to heighten any disagreement. He let his gait slow slightly, relaxing into the sway of the train, but his eyes stayed sharp across the faces of the patrons.

Money attracted people to the Rolling Dice, sure, but even temperate folks were drawn by the behemoth of innovation. Thirty-three cabins, two stories. Sleeper cabins up-top, recreation down below.

The upper tier was crowned with a dome of glass along each car and expansive windows, so passengers who could afford it had the luxury of sleeping under the stars and watching the landscape go by.

Below, the atmosphere was not so serene. A majority of the train's span was dedicated to the gamut of indulgences. Lounges, full-size bars with kitchens serving the finest foods one could imagine. The heart of this entertainment was the gambling dens. Amidst the clatter of chips and the murmur of negotiations, fortunes were risked over high-stakes deals. Some won, most lost, and the Dice never left a station empty.

He got through the first car without any incident and slid open the door to the next car. This one held game tables as well, but one entire side was taken up by a bar and high stools for for those between games.

"Read 'em and weep, boys!" exclaimed a boisterous gambler just as Corey slid into the car. He rocked his chair back on two legs, gloating his victory, but abruptly righted himself and gave a curt nod as Corey appeared. Others turned to look at him, and there was a brief dip in the car's energy.

Corey understood that, and gave them all a lopsided smile and a short nod. Weapons weren't allowed on the Dice, so the nightstick immediately signaled him as a guard. On paper, it was his job to maintain the integrity of the tables and make sure no patrons were cheated out of their hard-earned cash, but in practice he primarily trawled for card-counters and appeared when fists were flying to do his own bit of violence before escorting the offenders off the train.

"Last rooms! Last few rooms, all there is 'til next loop." The bartender deftly poured and drink and sent it down the bar, talking all the while. "Miss, it

can't be helped. Two rooms, that's all there is—
filling up! Cash won't make no difference."

The train had two lower cabins in the last two
cars of the train. They'd originally been game
rooms, like this one, but over time were
frequented less and less, then repurposed into
budget cabins to draw in poorer folk, but without
the signature luxury of the upper cabins, the dust
and cobwebs eventually took over. Now, they
were mostly storage, and though the bartender
promised it, they weren't likely open for booking.

The next car was a lounge, full of cigar smoke
and gauzy white curtains over the windows. It was
quieter in here, and the lounges were less likely to
have any trouble anyway, so Corey took a second
to stop and enjoy the silhouettes of the familiar
Hamilton streaming by outside.

He often played a sort of game with himself: if
the train was suddenly derailed, and it was up to
him to survive and make his own way back to
civilization, could he do it?

Here, he certainly could. Hamilton was his
childhood home, and he could make his way to it
from miles away, even in the dark. At night, the
city shone like a beacon, and he'd spent enough
years wandering in and around the city as a child,
he might even welcome the chance to walk
through it all again.

On the eastward side of the train
tracks however, lay a more perilous landscape.

Rocky fields stretched out toward the foothills and daunting cliffs of Mount Ulrich, which meant the train made a wide berth around the mountain and swung through the Dawn Plains , where the ground leveled off, and track could be laid more easily.

 He set o ff again, enjoying reminiscing about the land he'd grown up on. East of the tracks were two of the most significant plantations he'd ever heard of. The BrownCreeks owned the largest cotton plantation in the country and made sure everyone knew it. The Whitleys didn't own so much land, but in the early days of the nation their family were one of the biggest supporters of the Colonization Society and had replaced hundreds of freed slaves. Once that had filled their coffers, they pivoted to investing and had accumulated still more wealth by way of the railroads and shipping companies. If they hadn't build the tracks themselves, they'd funded the companies that had, and so they became synonymous with infrastructure across the nation. The Rolling Dice itself had the Whitleys to thank not only for its cars and steam engine, but also for the track it sped along.

About fifteen years before, when Corey was much younger and not yet working the train, the two families had come together and announced they'd captured Lightning in a Bottle, which served as both the name of their invention and the company they formed to market it. "Manageable light" they called it–safe and contained in glass like a lantern. They started spreading their bottled lightning in Hamilton and the other towns under Mount Ulrich, quickly replacing the old oil streetlamps.

The technical process behind their functionality had been relayed to Corey years ago, but the detail had long faded with the lights' novelty. Lightning in a Bottle quickly proved to be fraught with maintenance challenges. They were notorious for buzzing and flickering, and sometimes the glass would burst, sending sparks onto every nearby surface. After the fire departments declared they could no longer keep up, bottled lightning was restricted to outdoor use, and then only the streetlamps, which were far enough from buildings to prevent catching fire or lose sleep.

Just as the BrownCreeks and the Whitleys were scrambling to save their dying reputations, the Hodges Electric Company appeared on the scene. Their street lights might've buzzed, but they never burst, and the coated copper wires strung between each light meant no more need for the lamplighters to go to each pole one-by-one.

The Hodges Plantation in NimblePine even switched all their lights over to the new electric bulbs first, to show everyone else how safe and effective they were. Soon, the name Hodges was known far and wide around NimblePine to

Hamilton, and even beyond that. They were praised for the reliability and safety, and soon the gold standard for in-home lighting was Hodges Electric and no other.

But they didn't stop there. Doctor Hodges, the founder of their company and patriarch of the Hodges family, soon revealed his new invention: the flashlight. It was designed to be portable and used for short periods of time in the place of wired bulbs. Then, not only were homes and businesses filled with the light of Hodges Electric, but so were the fields, mines, and forests. Now that light could be cast anywhere, work hours extended beyond sunset.

The soft sound of violin music wafted through the air. For Corey, these moments were the highlights of his patrols: the music brought a sense of peace amidst the constant motion. This lounge in particular was known as the Mini Tavern, but was perhaps the most comfortable and least tavern-like of them, with lowered lighting and soft, live music by only a musician or two at a time. All of the plush chairs and sofas and low little tables were arranged so no matter where you sat, you had a good view of the passing scenery, and servers were under strict instructions to keep themselves as unnoticeable as possible as they passed back and forth.

Corey stepped to the side to let a server pass him, wondering at the way the man didn't stop or slow down but instead barrelled ahead with his tray of dinner service, nearly clipping Corey with it. He flicked a nod at the man and didn't recognize him, realizing why he might not know the train's etiquette.

The Dice had a high turnover rate for a number of reasons—chefs found under their benches, as inebriated as the passengers, waiters taking cuts of games, dealers rigging games. Vices were all too available on the Dice, and new hires often found themselves ensnared by them, perpetuating a cycle of misconduct and dismissal. The Dice was a nasty place, Corey often thought, and stayed well away from any untoward business.

Starting off again, Corey passed a man slumped over two chairs, a brown blanket draped over him and his rigid gray hat askew on his head, sleeping off whatever excesses had overcome him. Corey made a note to tell the next shift, but didn't think much of it. Sleepy was better than rowdy any day, and so far the man seemed to have been able to keep his stomach. He'd be woken at the next stop and either ushered to a cabin or out onto the platform.

The next thing he saw did raise his hackles, perhaps more than the goings-on of the Dice normally did. One of the couches near the rear door was taken up by two men, and between them a young girl who couldn't have been more than 14. Her eyes were vacant but her mouth smiling, staring off into the middle distance, seemingly lost in thought. The man to her left caught Corey's eye and slung an arm over her shoulders, giving her a little shake and Corey a smirk as if to challenge him. The other resolutely avoided his gaze, but Corey passed on with a disgusted huff.

Despite his feelings on the matter, which were decidedly negative–he didn't approve of such abominable behavior and wondered how the girl had gotten on the train in the first place– he knew messing with the men would be seen as unprovoked. There was no surer way to be removed from the payroll than interfering with peaceful, paying patrons. He quickened his step and made another note to pay attention on his journey back through the train.

As he reached the rear door and turned to do a final visual sweep, a minute shudder seemed to run through the car, almost too quick to see. Every person, momentarily chilled or unsettled by something he couldn't see, all at once. He felt it pass through another server at the same time, brushing very close by with an empty tray, but no one missed a step and the violin continued on uninterrupted.

He looked closer, scanning the faces of everyone he could see, looking out the window to see if the train had hit a bump, but it was too dark to see. When he saw nothing, he turned to pulled the door open and was hit with the strange sensation of everyone in the car looking at him, again all at once, for half a second. The waiter, by now on the other end of the car, the two men, the young woman, even the man in the chair. It was as if he could feel each of their eyes on his back. That sent a shudder through him, and he quickly stepped through and closed the door behind, worried he had looked foolish standing in the open doorway like that.

Late at night, on the Rolling Dice, as patrons' inhibitions lowered, boldness and paranoia often walked hand-in-hand. Unease nestled in his thoughts, the clacking of the train's wheels now a disconcerting backdrop. He steadied himself, resting a hand on his nightstick, and quickened his pace. This car was vibrant with noise and movement, and he found himself jumping at each whoop of triumph.

As he moved deeper into the car, having to weave through the crowd, he began to catch glances of concern from people watching a game of darts. Two men were at the farthest of four dartboards. One was tall, rail-thin, and wore his obvious wealth on his sleeve. His friend, clearly overserved, was bellowing ever louder and gesturing wildly.

"Haha-ha! Th'greatest comeback'f all time!"

"As much as I would like to play, Simmons, and witness—no doubt—the comeback of the ages,

I'm beginning to grow tired." The tall man's voice was much quieter, but Corey was close enough now to hear, acutely aware of the crowd at his back. "We had best be off if we hope to eat tonight, my boy."

Reaching for another dart with unsteady hands, Simmons missed by a few inches and stumbled a step into the table, letting out an involuntary burp.

"M'cups're beginnin t'posses more a me th'n I'd like," he joked weakly.

His companion, who bore a striking scar across his right cheek and a youthful face framed by the shadow of a beard, gave a wry smile and gestured for them to move along. Simmons, immediately distracted by a passing woman, shot out a hand and slapped her across the rear, bellowing at the same time, "Ohhh, give us 'Th' Night Air B'gins t'Shine,' bartender!" Another burp, and an affronted gasp from the woman, who was quickly yanked away by a friend.

The noise had all but stopped, except for Simmons, who by then had noticed all the eyes on him and was bolstered by the attention.

"C'mon! Play th'music!" He laughed uproariously while his friend reached for the drink in his hand. He tried to gently steer Simmons physically away from the table, but Simmons wouldn't have it, and lunged for the darts again.

"Look at him, the fool! You'd think he was really getting married," Corey heard someone whisper just behind him and began to shoulder closer.

He emerged right next to the table and addressed the tall man, "Do you have a cabin you–"

"A challenger! C'mon! Las'time I came'way w'th more cash th'n I could hold. I would've a'gin I hadn't betted on Judy Lane!" Simmons swung an arm in a too-wide hook, aiming for Corey's throat, too drunk to be fast. Corey easily stepped out of range, and Simmons' momentum carried him forward, clipping one hip against the edge of the table and sending him crashing to the floor. The sharp crack of his palms hitting the wood sent a shot of guilt through Corey, even as he maintained a professional demeanor. The closest onlookers stumbled back as the cup of darts on the table went careening to the floor.

"I don't mean to be rude, sir, but can you please help me get him up?"

Corey reached down to haul Simmons up by one shoulder while his friend took the other, Simmons grumbling and dazed all the way.

"Excellent, I believe I've got him from here. We'll be on our way; this has been rather, ah" he paused, glancing around at the dispersing onlookers, "embarrassing is the word, I suppose." He chuckled, a hint of self-deprecation in his voice.

"I thought you might be."

Simmons attempted to lunge down again, seeing the spilled darts, but was stopped by Corey's arms still holding him upright. It was then that Corey saw his keys, a full step away under the table. He hadn't felt them leave his belt. He slapped one hand over the loop that normally held them to his belt, finding it open, and then swooped down to retrieve them. His keyring had never fallen off. He swung his head around to look behind him, mind immediately going to attempted theft, but no one was paying any more attention to him or the two men at the table. The din of talk and laughter was returning, and no one caught his eye as he swept the car.

The tall man now sidled up to Corey, Simmons leaning dazed on the table, his coat on. With a smooth gesture, he pulled a coin from his coat pocket, flicked it once into the air, caught it, and sent it spinning again toward Corey. The flash of gold was unmistakable in the dim cabin light.

"Archibald, and thank you, sir," he called as he turned and ushered Simmons toward the far door, presumably to find their cabins.

Corey caught the coin, the weight of the round gold coin was small but a significant token of thanks for his help, but he still bit into it to confirm it to be genuine. It was. Despite the earlier tension, the gesture added a feeling of closure, and even his earlier paranoia began to ebb. He awkwardly pocketed the gold coin and gave a stilted nod.

"Uh, thank you. Have a good one," he managed to say, but neither man turned.

Suddenly feeling heavy and somewhat dizzy, he fixed his eyes to the floor, which seemed to shift ever so slightly, sliding about beneath his feet.

"Coffee, please. Black." He stepped gingerly over to the bar and leaned on it for support.

"This your round over? The old bartender inquired, reaching for an already-brewed coffee pot.

"Not done, got two more cabins, then," he trailed off, grasping the cup handed to him and raising it in thanks.

The last two cars needed only a quick sweep, then he could make the long, tedious way back to the guard's cabin and settle in for a long wait.

They were storage—the two former sleeper cabins that had been converted to storage. There was a bathroom on either end that he ducked into, if only to see if there was anyone who had gotten lost and might need to be escorted back to the public cars.

Ducking out of the far bathroom, ready to glance into the nooks and crannies and get out of there, the floor began to move again, slipping as if someone was attempting to yank the carpet out from under him. He caught the wall with one hand and tried to steady himself, downing the last of the coffee for a moment of relief. However, with each step he took, the floor seemed to move more erratically beneath him, even while the car didn't so much as bounce.

His heart began to pound, his legs turning to jelly so he had to lean heavily on the wall. Employees on the Dice were equipped with a whistle for emergencies, and the guards were no exception. Desperation setting in, Corey fumbled in his coat to take his out, but was met with empty fabric. The little pocket sew into the left breast for exactly this purpose was empty.

He'd never had to use the whistle, never took it out, and it couldn't have fallen. Attempting to regain his bearings enough to shout, Corey pushed himself away from the wall, only to find that everything that had been on his right side, was now on his left, and the floor was rapidly rushing up to meet him. The last sound he heard was the jingle of his keys.

Kendall.
18??

The relentless sun bore down on Kendall, its rays unimpeded by the cloudless sky. Every step kicked up dust that hung in the hot air. The only shade around was a gnarled, nearly leafless tree, and she decided it was as good a time as any to take a break. Settling heavily against the trunk, her gaze fell on a procession of ants bustling below her. They moved in strange circles rather than the lines she would have expected, and she watched them swirl around and around without making progress.

Eva had unceremoniously secured and then ejected all of their escape pods after she'd managed to strap the dazed and flailing Oliver into his. Despite their protests, and Kendall's fruitless effort to free herself and help Eva to escape what was rapidly becoming a depressurization event, Eva had gotten to the button before her, and she could only watch in horror as the Dawn dwindled away and the ground came rushing closer and closer.

Training for this mission had been rigorous. She and the others were prepared for every scenario from injury to drought to contact with locals, but nothing could have prepared her for the mental strain of being alone in such a desolate place. Individual escape pods were more energy and cost-efficient, but they relied on the team to locate one-another and trek cross-country to reunite if they ever had to be deployed.

That was where she found herself: sitting under a tree that in other circumstances she would be identifying and collecting samples from, no way of knowing where the others' pods had landed, if they had at all, and what had become of Eva.

The air was thick with an occasional breeze that shifted the humidity around but offered no relief. Kendall took a deep breath, appreciating the scent of dirt and wood after so much time in the sterile air of the Dawn. She knew she had to keep moving, find clear water, find food and shelter. Alone and dangerously dehydrated, she couldn't help but brood over her circumstances. What had once been a new and exciting adventure was now a living nightmare, and she was now faced with the very real possibility of never making it out of this alien environment alive.

Her survival kit was getting critically low. The initial three-day ration was depleted much faster than anticipated, having to keep up with the aches and pains of post-pod flight and landing as well as the lack of any viable natural resources. She still had water purification tablets, but had yet to find even a mud puddle to use them in.

She scanned the horizon once more, searching for any sign of water, but the landscape offered no mercy—no stream or pond, only endless vistas of dry earth in every direction. With each passing moment, her hope dwindled.

Finally, she pushed herself stiffly to her feet and headed for a set of foothills far in the distance. After what seemed like a never-ending stretch of dry earth, she began to encounter a few trees and coarse shrubs. They seemed in a constant struggle between life and decay: some trees stood tall and robus with dark, hard bark and branches, their leaves green and dense exactly as they appeared in her training data. But others were contorted and misshapen, looking like they had sprung out of a surrealist painting rather than something natural. Their bark was spongy and flaked off easily when she ran her fingers across it.

Together, it created a deep sense of unease as she continued to search for water, even stopping occasionally to listen for it.

She reached the top of a hill and began to descend the other side. The vegetation thickened the further she descended, still in its strange pattern of disease, until the underbrush was clawing at her ankles and calves. She couldn't see far ahead anymore, and her legs were beginning to feel made of lead.

However, she had to admit it was exciting to get to see this new side of Earth. She began identifying the trees and plants she passed to distract herself, taking note of the tall and increasingly abundant oaks, the firs and pines and even the trees she couldn't identify, filing them away for later.

She walked until her feet throbbed and she could barely lift her feet to go on. In a small valley, she found another tree with a wide patch of moss under it and slid down gratefully to sit. It was cooler here, and the abundant shelter meant the sun was no longer beating down at the top of her head.

"Where am I going?" she said aloud, momentarily letting the frustration get the best of her. Then, she sat in silence for a long while and breathed.

What would she do if she couldn't find any of the other crew? She couldn't be expected to live out the rest of her days here, even if she could find a town. And even if she did find the others, they were still trapped here. The only way to communicate back to mission control was on the Dawn, which could be in any number of pieces floating up in space. Were any of the others even alive? Were they looking for her?

A branch snapped out in front of her, and leaves rustled, getting closer. A shot of adrenaline shot through her when she realized it was footsteps—a large animal. Something was approaching, and quickly, and it would pass directly by her. Kendall scrambled behind the tree she had been leaning against, hoping its girth would conceal her long enough to form a plan.

She scanned her surroundings, looking for any potential hiding places. Her eyes caught sign of a small, dark opening at the base of a nearby hill, partially hidden by overgrown bushes. The footsteps continued to get closer, and she dashed toward the shelter, careful to keep her steps as light as possible and her head low. The little cave had just enough space to hide her out of sight, and she shoved herself as far into it as she could.

Pressing herself against the cool earth around her, she kept her ears and eyes trained outside, muscles tense and ready to fight or flee. But as the animal came through the trees, the creaking of leather joined its footsteps, and a little ways away Kendall could begin to see a man on horseback. She didn't recognize him, but relief washed over her anyway. She couldn't help but wonder who he might be, and whether he might be friendly enough to help her, but she stayed still and silent.

The moments stretched on, and the man and his horse faded into the distance. Still, she waited, counting the seconds to ensure he was truly gone.

She shifted to lay flat, her body stiff from the tension and chill. A traveler likely meant a settlement was nearby, but if he hadn't met anyone else, that probably meant the Dawn crew weren't anywhere close.

The desire to call out for Mia or Alison was overwhelming. Part of her thought that she could have been wrong, and they were just beyond the trees, hiding like she had been and would soon reveal themselves. But fear of attracting the wrong attention kept her silent. It would be safer to find a house or town than to ask a strange man for help in the wilderness.

As the light dwindled, Kendall stared at the fading sun through the leaves, her thoughts drifting between hope and despair. Eventually, exhaustion took over, and she drifted into a restless sleep haunted by the mission's events and the uncertainty of what lay ahead.

She woke early, abrupt and unsettling. Her arms and neck itched fiercely. She looked down and discovered that she was covered in bugs, and she nearly hit her head on the ceiling of the cave jumping up and flailing her arms and legs to dislodge them. Once the initial shock subsided and she managed to calmly brush the last of them off, she took a moment to inspect her skin. Surprisingly, there were no bites or allergic reactions, just the lingering sensation of tiny legs and antennae. With a mixture of relief and disgust, she chuckled at the absurdity of her situation.

"Bugs, ha," she murmured, crouching down to get a closer look at them.

Their diversity was astounding–shiny beetles, multiple species of ant, some insect with menacing pincers. She lost count of the varieties, each more peculiar than the last.

She stood back up with a shudder, shaking stragglers off of her boots and bag. They, like the ants the previous day, moved in ways she wasn't prepared for. After their initial scramble away from her, they organized themselves into neat, single-file lines back into the dark corners of the cave or out into the underbrush. There didn't seem to be any difference in how the different species behaved except that some could fly and seemed more inclined to take to the air in orderly clumps while the rest trundled through the dirt.

As a botanist, her knowledge of plants was far more extensive than any other scientific training, but even she knew that this wasn't how bugs normally behaved. She gathered herself to set out into the forest, wondering what might be driving such behavior.

Stepping out of the cave, the heat of the sun immediately hit her. It was already high and the day was stifling even in the shade. Realizing she had missed much of her chance to follow the traveler's tracks and had gone yet another day without adequate food or water, she did her best to stretch out the discomfort of sleeping on the cave floor. She couldn't afford to lose time like this. She would have to conserve energy that day to avoid oversleeping again.

Just then, more rustling and snapping sticks came from the hillside, then muffled voices. She crouched back into the brush covering the cave's entrance and froze, listening. The forest seemed to hold its breath along with her, the usual sounds of wildlife eerily absent.

She summoned the energy to inch back into the cave, careful not to make a single sound. She hoped they might just be travelers, like the man on horseback, or that they could be from the same town, and maybe it was much closer than she thought.

Pushing through the underbrush, she discovered it had covered a smaller entrance just inside the larger one, which led further back into pitch darkness. She stepped into it, careful not to go too far, and heard the voices sound again.

"You check! I'm not going in there." The voice was raspy and hoarse, but held a tinge of familiarity that Kendall didn't have time to examine.

She tried to step further into the darkness, but the passage narrowed too much to go any further. She was trapped in the secondary cave with only a thin veil of darkness between her and discovery. The footsteps halted right outside the cave.

"Hello?" A man called out. Kendall's skin tingled with fear. She closed her eyes, praying he would turn back. Her hands slid along the cave floor, looking for anything that might serve as a weapon, and came upon a stone large enough to lift in both hands.

She couldn't imagine hitting anyone with it, but reality was quickly bearing down on her. She would hit him, she decided, and run. She wouldn't be taken prisoner, she wouldn't stay and fight.

"Come on," the raspy voice said, and the cadence of the voice made Kendall pause. It was a woman's voice, and she could have sworn she'd heard it before. "This one doesn't look big enough. We need to keep moving.

Just then, a man's head and arm roughly thrust themselves through the brush concealing her. She barely had time to raise the stone over her head before his hand closed over her wrist.

"Woah! It's just me!" That's when she recognized him, his face half-illuminated by the sun and his voice clear and loud.

Oliver let her arm go and held the brush to the side so she could see Eva standing behind him, looking frustrated.
"Come on, Ken. We gotta go."

Sam

1861

"Alright boys, you all are headed for Emerald Ranch," the overseer who had introduced himself as Jacob growled. "You'll be known as scarabs. The journey's long, but easy. Should be simple."

The newly bought men all nodded. Sam cut his eyes back and forth between their faces. Most of them were downcast, filled with the weight of their fate. He saw himself reflected in their despair.

There was a long pause, then another of the overseers stood up and sighed. "Alright. Before you proceed, you have to understand and follow Emerald Ranch's rules." He raised one finger. "Rule one: respect the hierarchy. We've got managers, aunts, uncles. Everybody has a role. Learn 'em. Respect 'em. There are a few Big Daddy's out and about." He paused and seemed to reconsider. "But we can get to those in a minute. Moral is, know your place."

Sam was familiar with rules and hierarchies, but he'd never had them announced to him before. Usually, he was thrown into a new environment and expected to figure it out on his own.

Jacob and two other men sat in the front of the wagon, one of them driving while the other two had taken down the curtain behind the driver's seat and were turned to address them.

"Rule two—and our most important—" he raised his voice to be heard by all. Sylvester Hodges and the auction were becoming a distant memory. The sky had begun to shift to to darker colors, and the first stars were appearing through cracks in the wagon's roof.

They trundled on, the overseers sitting slumped against the sides of the driver's seat, lazily observing them all. Something on Sam's face must have caught Jacob's attention, because his eyes didn't leave Sam's face as he finished rule two, "Any form of rebellion or questioning of authority is strictly forbidden."

This was also all too familiar to Sam. It seemed that Emerald Ranch, despite its friendly name and strangely casual owner, would be no different than any other. He carefully held his face in a neutral expression and lowered his gaze.

"Conformity ensures peace and stability," continued Jacob, adding some enthusiasm into his voice. "It's simple! Any attempt to escape—any—

leads to punishment. Failure to comply means…" he trailed off and gestured for the men to finish his sentence. When none did, he shook his head and leaned forward. "Failure to comply means severe consequences."

The silence that followed was thicker than before, filled with the heavy breaths of men accepting and contemplating their circumstance. Rules were chains that bound them tighter than any physical shackle ever could, and they slumped low under their weight.

"Ahh, come on, you all know this." Jacob punctuated his sentence with a noisy tobacco spit, the dark juice staining the wood just over a chained man's shoulder. "Accept it. Might be a little easier," he added gruffly, then slapped both hands on top of his knees and turned, yanking the curtain shut behind him.

The overseers voices rose again after a moment, laughing and talking with one-another about nothing in particular.

Sam let himself sink down, fixing his eyes to the passing plains. He thought resolutely of the future, determined not to let Emerald Ranch claim him. He would still escape someday, alone this time, and set off North.

"That's as stupid as anything," one of the men whispered, his head bent to talk with Lewis to Sam's right. The sun had finished its descent, and the only lights were the wagon's lanterns and that distant flame. The overseers were still talking and laughing uproariously. Sam sighed and leaned carefully against the back rail of the wagon. He gazed up at the vast sea of stars, trying to tune out the murmuring that had cropped up in Lewis' direction.

"Have you ever asked yourself—think about it—after all this traveling you've done—you ever asked yourself where we're at? Where are we in this country?" Lewis' voice was barely audible, still full of its trademark curiosity, but marred with hints of desperation.

"Why's that important?" one of the men replied, his expression baffled. Sam smiled to himself.

Lewis, undeterred, pressed on, "Me and you—where are we. There's us, and white people, and we've see Indians and others, too, right?" He received a reluctant nod.

"So, where do we fit in with all of them, ya know?"

"Who knows. You're making my head hurt." The man did his best to shuffle away from Lewis in the crowded wagon, earning grumbles and a few halfhearted shoves from the men around him.

In typical Lewis fashion, as if the man had never spoken at all, Lewis rambled on.

"An easier question is to ask yourself, where do we sit in the history of the country? I mean, look at everything that's been made. It's all been by us or the white people." He paused, waiting for a response. "That means we fit somewhere, obviously. It's kinda like if the country was a picture, then we're the frame, you know? Maybe this house is not our home."

"Not our home," Sam found himself echoing softly, the words settling within him.

"That's right!" Lewis said, drawing dirty looks when he voice rose a little too much for secrecy. "It's a saying I heard when I was a little house worker." Sam waited for Lewis to elaborate, which he did after a thoughtful pause. "Meaning a home ain't always a house."

While Lewis was talking, the wagon came rocking to a stop. The overseers dismounted, and there was a moment while they paced and spoke among themselves.

Jacob appeared at the back of the wagon. "We'll camp here for the night," he said.

They waited a while longer while Jacob and the others gathered wood and set up their bedrolls. When the fire was crackling and warm, they were permitted to sit and talk quietly amongst themselves around it, their chains removed for the time being. They passed water and food among themselves and tried to find comfortable places to lie in the dust. The overseers sat in their own group around their own fire, taking shifts watching over the scarabs.

Sam did his best to get comfortable and was dozing to the sound of the fire when a sound off in the darkness roused him. He sat up and found that the others had as well, looking in all directions for the source of the noise. Lewis, ever at Sam's side, was not paying any such attention. Seeing Sam move, he held out a half-empty can.

"You want these—"

"What was that?" Sam asked, just loud enough for the group around him to hear. A few shook their heads or shrugged, others started murmuring and gesturing one direction or another.

Another crack sounded, this time loud enough to be a whole limb or rotten trunk. The overseers were standing now, calling across the fire for everyone to settle down.

Suddenly, a nearby tree branch shook violently, and a bird burst forth, flapping frantically into the night. Some of the scarabs chuckled nervously, relieved, but Sam gathered himself. Something big had scared that bird.

Then, there was a faint tickling along the top of one of his feet, and he looked down to see a procession of black beetles branching out along the ground beneath them. He shook them off, and in shifting his feet crushed several, but the others kept scuttling along toward the fire.

"Who's there!" Jacob yelled. All of the overseers had picked up their guns and were stumbling in various states of drunkenness to order the scarabs to sit back down, many of them having stood to see what was coming.

"What's that smell?" said Lewis. Sam could smell it too. It was pungent, thick with a sour tang. It coated his tongue and the back of his throat, making bile rise. He pulled the collar of his shirt up to cover his nose.

"There!" Someone yelled, pointing over Sam's left shoulder toward where the bird had come. A huge black shape could barely be seen lumbering through the trees, too far out of the fire light to be seen clearly. They were all on their feet then, backing away while the overseers yelled over them and tried to shove some to the ground.

The night erupted into chaos. The creature, moving faster than Sam could have imagined, lunged toward the closest scarab, crashing right through the branches and brush in its way. A humming came with it, and Sam found himself desperately swatting hundreds of flying bugs out of his face, feeling them crawl over his feet and up his legs, land on his arms and shoulders, all the while trying to get as far away from the beast as the overseers would allow.

It was a bear, its fur matted and wet with something black, its mouth open to reveal broken and yellowed teeth. It swiped short of the scarab, who was yanked back by others as they scattered. Sam saw it land on all fours and swing its head around to survey them, its eyes gleaming with firelight, its snout covered in moving, writhing insects. He turned and ran.

A shot went off from one of the overseers' guns, the bullet embedding itself in a tree with a thud. Sam passed a few scarabs who remained frozen to the spot, their eyes fixed on the monstrous bear. He tried to shove a few into movement, but most stumbled or fell. Only one saw Sam's face and seemed to come back to himself, taking off into the dark in a different direction.

Sam ran until all he could see was darkness, tripping over rocks and tree roots, raising his own racket in his haste. He could hear the screams of the men behind him and the report of guns, even the terrible roar of the bear that turned his legs to rubber. The humming had receded behind him, and now he only felt the occasional brush of insects colliding with his body. A few others ran past him, and he swung around expecting to be attacked, but nothing came. He looked back once, and saw the bear lunge again but couldn't see who through the trees.

Stumbling along, he swept his hands out around him until he found a tree he thought he could climb, and scrambled up it, nearly falling several times on the way up. He climbed as far as the strength of the branches would allow, and then sat there, breathing hard and holding tight to the trunk. He shut his eyes tight and listened as the screams and crashing waned. Then there was just the bear, shuffling around and flattening the brush, and then it was quiet again.

He clung there for hours longer, waiting for the bear to sniff him out and come climbing up the tree. His body ached and his legs and palms burned where he had scraped them on the bark. To avoid nodding off, he recited every name he knew, all the towns he'd ever been to, all the songs and stories he could remember, and finally the sky began to gray and lighten, and he could see that the bear was nowhere around.

Cautiously, he descended from the tree and slunk away from the dead fire and back toward the road. As he emerged, a movement and a soft call from the opposite side caught his attention.

"Who's there?" He whispered, eyes still darting around him to ensure nothing was waiting to ambush him.

A man rose from behind a thicket of bushes, stumbled a step or two, and fell out of sight again. As Sam drew closer, he saw Lewis lying there, battered and bleeding, but alive. Lewis raised a hand and grimaced.

"You're alive." In awe, Sam knelt down to help Sam sit up, propping him up against a fallen trunk.

Lewis squeezed his eyes shut and let his head fall back against the wood. "Eh, barely."

Jimmy
1872

Jimmy leaned against the wall, staring through the window and the moon glow at Mount Ulrich. The clattering of wheels against iron tracks echoed through the car.

"Anytime now," he ground out under his breath. Waiting was far from his favorite pass-time. He pulled out his watch and followed the second hand's progress with his eyes.

Promptly as it passed the three, he heard a groan, sliding, and then a thud on the other side of the door. He cracked it and peeked out to see the security guard sprawled unmoving on the floor.

Satisfied, he threw the door the rest of the way open and stepped out. The Moon Shadow gang had a reputation as a formidable and efficient organization, and he was happy to play his part in that, if not always to sit quietly and wait for his turn.

Their research indicated that the Dice, though famously wealthy, had a few secrets left in its recesses. For all the cash they waved in the gaming rooms, Simmons insisted there were more riches to be had in the two decommissioned lower cabins. He'd heard word of gold and other valuables smuggled in flatware crates to further pad the purses of the train's owners.

Simmons had been on the train for a few days by then, posing as a customer and carrying out his part of the plan. Probably taking full advantage of the open bars, too. Jimmy hoped he'd been able to keep his wits about him. Demolitions were better handled sober, and so much rode on the pre-agreed placements of all the charges Simmons had smuggled in his bags.

Jimmy moved smoothly to the far door of the cabin, swaying with the soothing rock of the train. He pulled the door open fluidly and made a beeline for the stacks of crates in the last cabin. A thrill went through him. His phase had so far been a rousing success. He needed only to confirm the whereabouts of the treasure and give the rest of the team the go-ahead and they'd be off. If he found nothing, well, he'd never liked Simmons that much anyway.

He tried the tops of a few crates and trunks before he found one loose enough to begin to pry off, then found a loose board and used it to lever the lid onto the floor.

There they were, under a few layers of straw filling: rows and rows of gold bars, each one gleaming in the pale light of the moon.

"Here we go," he said to the quiet cabin, then replaced the lid loosely on top of the crate and returned to the public cars.

The first he saw was Sherane, perched strategically at a bar table to see him as he came through. He gave her a short nod and two fingers to the brim of his hat, not slowing his stride. Her eyes blazed.

He found Juelz a few cars down, plainly clothed and bare-faced, slumped under a ratty gray blanket. Jimmy passed close enough to kick one of his legs a little harder than he'd meant to, then stopped and leaned over to apologize when he bolted up, disgruntled.

"My apologies sir, I must watch where I'm going." And off he was again, politely stepping out of the way of servers, dealers, and other customers, always headed for the front of the train.

With every new car and subtle signal, his anticipation ratcheted up. They'd rehearsed this meticulously, planned and argued, choreographed everything to the smallest detail. He sometimes found himself walking faster than a leisurely customer out to order dinner might be and had to slow himself to a plod, carefree smile firmly fixed to his face.

He got to Max and Kenny, stopped to sneeze so they could offer him a hanky, and then they excused themselves from their table to turn in for the night and disappeared ahead of him. He declined to take their place and plead a growling stomach, keeping himself moving so no over-enthusiastic gamblers could get ahold of him.

Max and Kenny were to race ahead to the front of the train and subtly subdue the telegraph operator. Part of Jimmy hoped it might not turn out so subtle. He often thought the more violent option, while unsavory, was cleaner. No need to maintain a hostage who might at any moment give them away, but that wasn't their way, and anyway, there'd be enough chaos from other sources.

He reached a tavern car fourth from the front and claimed an open stool at the bar. The bartender approached a moment later, cleaning a glass. Jimmy ordered two shots of whiskey, and they appeared in front of him a moment later, but before he could raise one, a series of shots rang out in the cabin above. He felt his teeth grind against one-another. That would be Archie and an awkward, though not catastrophic, mistake.

Jimmy dropped to the floor along with the rest of the car's inhabitants and saw Juelz crawling toward him. They locked eyes and Jimmy gave a short nod. Dancing as one, he and Juellz drew their firearms and climbed to their feet, Juelz going to bar the door to the back of the train and Jimmy taking a few long strides to reach the middle of the car.

"All right! Everybody sit the fuck down!" Juelz gave a short look.

"Actually, get the fuck up against the wall!"

Together, they were able to wrangle almost everyone against the same wall with only a few bruises and black eyes on those who didn't comply fast enough. When they were done, three men remained seated at a card table, all of their faces still as stone.

A commotion came from the stairwell to the second floor and Archie appeared, immediately giving Jimmy and Juelz a pained, apologetic glance.

"I do believe you three don't have any brains." Juelz sauntered over to the table and pressed the muzzle of his sidearm to the temple of one man's head. "Up you get."

A woman lunged out of the lineup, "Who in the hell do you—"

She cut off with a gasp as Jimmy swung around to block her path, then nodded ruefully in Archie's direction. It took her a moment, but eventually she turned to see the barrel of Archie's gun pointed right between her eyebrows.

"That's a nice dress you have on, ma'am, but this young man here'll gladly dress you in a halo if you don't get back up against that fuckin' wall." Jimmy kept his voice low and gentle, letting the words themselves impact with their full weight. As she was doing as she was told, one of the men at the table, who had been hiding a glass bottle in his lap, raised it and struck it against the corner of the table, swinging the now razor edge at Juelz. He didn't even get halfway before Juelz pistol went off and he fell to the floor, splattering Juelz, the other two men, and the floor with his blood.

Jimmy scanned the passengers' faces. "Anyone else?" They all avoided his eye, and he took out his watch to check the time.

"Anchor up." Juelz gestured to the two men still at the table. "Eh, leave 'em." Juelz shrugged, gave one man a last shove, and backed off.

He and Archie went to opposite doors to brace themselves, and Jimmy wedged himself behind the bar while the other passengers looked on in confusion and fear. They didn't have to wait long before the train gave a mighty shake and began to rapidly slow. The suddenness wrenched Jimmy's shoulder something awful, and he was peppered with falling bottles of booze, but that was nothing compared to the passengers, who went sprawling on top of one another to the floor, under tables, against the side of the bar.

Shortly, they came to a shuddering stop, and Jimmy leapt into action. He slid a bandana over his mouth and nose and rushed past Archie to the third car, where Sherane was blending into her own chaos among the lounge chairs. He brandished his weapon and hauled her to her feet as gently as he could, given the circumstances, and tapped the barrel of the gun to the side of her head. For her part, her shriek was as believable as anything, as were the trembling hands she raised.

He pushed her toward the front of the car, already anticipating the commotion in car two. He positioned them with a few chairs and cowering passengers between them and the door, and in another moment a crowd of guards with guns shoved themselves through it.

"Bad idea, you piece of shit," one guard growled. He glanced at Sherane, then back at Jimmy.

Jimmy waited until they had all come through the door, watched it close behind them, and pulled deftly at a band across the back of Sherane's shoulders. She raised her arms. And the rotating barrels of two machine guns emerged from the sleeves beneath her hands. By the time the guards figured out the fire was coming from the hostage, they'd already been wounded or shot down. When the guns in her sleeves clicked empty, Sherane lifted her mink scarf's head from her shoulder and squeezed a place behind its front legs. Bullet after bullet exploded from its mouth one at a time while Jimmy shot over her shoulder until every guard lay motionless.

When the gunfire ceased, a figure began to climb through a shattered window and Jimmy nearly fired his own gun at it before realizing it was Steve, his scarred, boyish face coming into view beneath the frame. He planted his feet and adjusted his long, fine brown coat. Together with Sherene, they stepped over the bodies of the guards, leaving crying, shell-shocked passengers behind them, and emerged into the lead car.

They found nothing but an empty security office and two black men huddled at the far end. One had a scarred face, but both wore the fine clothes of the Dice's two proprietors.

They didn't put up a fight and were easily tied up and stowed in a corner while Jimmy, Sherene, and Steve exchanged triumphant looks and went to make themselves comfortable in the empty chairs.

They got a few good minutes of gloating and congratulating each other on their jobs-well-done when Simmons burst through the door, nearly throwing himself to the floor in his haste. He looked up, his face red and pupils large.

"Simmons," Steve said sourly, "What the hell are you doing here?"

"Pinkertons," Simmons panted, the syllables heavy and slow in his mouth.

They all froze, and Simmons, frustrated with their lack of action, gathered himself to bellow again: "Pinkertons!"

Lewis

1861

All around him, men screamed and moaned in fear and pain. Lewis lay there, still as he could, listening to their cries dwindle and stop and wondering if he, too, was dying. The trees blurred, and then the sky turned red and wet.

And then Sam appeared as if out of heaven and helped him slow the bleeding. Then he was gone again and came back with the wagon and one of the horses, which reared and pulled at the rope he'd tied around its head. Being lifted into the wagon hurt, and sitting propped against the back of the driver's seat hurt, and he breathed hard and ragged. His head felt seconds from bursting, and one eye remained swollen shut and so painful he eventually had to close the other—like ice picks digging into him.

"Maybe—maybe they'll hang me," he had to pause to draw a wheezing lungful of air, "behind a building somewhere—somewhere quiet."

He could see Sam shaking his head out of the corner of his eye, but, "Don't think like that," was all he said. And then they rode on, the horse's hooves thudding rhythmically, the wagon creaking and bouncing. Sam wasn't a bad driver, but the horse was clearly tired and jumped at every fluttering leaf. They swerved and several times nearly ended up stuck, but on they went for days, always camping well off the road, never building fire for warmth or to heat the untouched cans left in the back of the wagon.

Lewis didn't mention the bear. He hoped Sam would, but he only ever talked about heading north, staying moving, keeping out of town. Lewis knew bears sometimes came into camps looking for food, but he also knew that hadn't been any ordinary visit. Faced with guns, fire, a crowd of men all up and moving about, most bears would have given up and run away. Even if it attacked, it wouldn't rip through a group like that. Bears were smart, like people. They didn't pick unnecessary fights.

And then those bugs—all over his body, flying into his mouth as he screamed, hundreds of them squishing beneath his running feet.

They did as Sam said: headed North. No destination in mind. Lewis wondered if they would keep driving north forever, through the trees and the mountains, and then the snow and ice all the way to the top of the world. Lewis wasn't overly fond of the cold, but he did think it might be nice to see the arctic once, now that he could choose his own way.

"You have a plan?" said Sam. Most of Lewis' aches and pains had calmed enough for him to sit beside Sam in the driver's seat, but the brightness of the sun during the day made his head throb, so he still sat in the back during the worst of it.

Sam half-turned to look at him, expecting an answer.

A bump jolted Lewis' head against a board, and he winced. "'Course I do. If we're gonna be free, we may as well toss the dice, huh?"

"Say we get over those hills. Then what?"

"Oh, a featherbed," Lewis gave a short chuckle, "for a start. Then we get to work. Trains don't buy themselves."

Sam nodded gravely and was silent again, urging the horse a little faster.

They followed the twisting, turning road for a long time until Lewis noticed a rustling in the trees they passed. The horse puffed and stopped abruptly, jolting them both forward in their seats. Sam snapped the rains at it, but it only danced a few steps to the side and stood perfectly still again, its ears pointed high and its body rigid.

"Stupid horse," Sam roared, swinging the reins frantically over the horse's back.

Lewis looked in the same direction, scanning the trees, disbelieving that they could have been caught so quickly and without any warning.

More rustling. Sam noticed this time and stopped his raging. It came again, this time on the other side of the road. The horse sidestepped again. For half a second, Lewis could have sworn he heard something above them, but immediately dismissed it.

"We could hop on the horse, give it a kick." He whispered at Sam, feeling the urgent need to act. Sam considered for a moment, and the horse whinnied, high and urgent.

"Fuck," he heard Sam say under his breath, then Sam tapped the reins against the horse's back one more time before giving up and dropping them to the floor of the driver's seat.

"He-ey, did you hear that?" A sing-songy, almost gleeful voice called above them. Then low, giggling laughter.

"There!" another hissed, and both Sam and Lewis jolted and tried to stand up.

"What do you think?" Came a deep, lazy man's voice from the shadows.

"Eh, I don't know," said the first voice, followed by a chorus of agreement.

The murmuring seemed to come from all around them, even under their feet below the wagon, and they constantly whipped back and forth, trying to catch the owner of each voice.

"Could be worker bees, ehh, two of 'em," a voice suggested.

"Too raggedy for poachers. But, mm, still. Could be poachers."

"Does it matter?"

"They have a horse."

At that moment, panic claimed Lewis, and he bolted without a second thought. With all he had, he sprinted through the darkening woods. There was a soft rustle and creak above and beside him, as if the forest itself were alive. Branches and thorns tore at his clothes and limbs. He startled at shadows and frantically changed his course once, twice, before stumbling over a rotting, fallen tree. He scrambled to press his back against it, clapping a hand over his mouth to muffle ragged, strained breaths.

The sudden snap of a stick behind his head jolted him into motion again, and he sprang to his feet only to see a bird flap up from the log. Relieved, he looked around once and then sunk to hide behind the log again.

He'd left Sam. Shame and guilt came crashing in so forcefully he almost stood and ran back the way he'd came. He was all alone out there, and so was Sam either captured or escaped too, but both with little hope of finding the other again.

He bent his head to bury in his hands, and a hand clamped down on his bicep, firm but not painful.

"Gotcha," a voice snarled. Lewis twisted and tried to dislodge the hand. "We didn't do it! It was a bear! Honest, we were going to go back!" Barely aware of what he was saying, Lewis gave up fighting to cower on the forest floor.

The man grunted, then used both hands to haul Lewis up and over the log, forcing him back toward the road. "You'll be comin' with us."

Kendall.
18??

Kendall's steps were unsteady as she, Oliver, and Eva made their way up the hill. Exhaustion clouded her senses, but it didn't dampen the thrill of discovery.

"We're actually here. In the Heartland," she marveled aloud. The other two nodded and made sounds of agreement but were preoccupied with their climb.

At the summit, she paused, feeling as though she could see the entire world from that vantage point. Below, the landscape of green stretched endlessly, thousands of acres of forest merging with the horizon. To the north, the terrain transitioned to wide, rolling hills ribboned with thin tributaries headed to the distant river. Behind those hills loomed the larger, more imposing shapes of mountains with Mount Ulrich at their head. To the west, the trees gave way to tall, fluttering prairie grasses shining gold in the sunlight. They stood for a moment and watched it ripple like water in the wind.

Eastward was East Winden, marked by dense forest barrier between them and the majority of the country's population. They intended neither to enter East Winden nor to pass through it, especially now when their situation was so precarious. The only thing so far that had kept the group's sanity intact was Eva's surety and determination, which she displayed in that moment, breaking through Kendall's reverie.

"We need to get to Bridgewater. I remember northwest."

Oliver swept his gaze over the vista again, squinting at this and that. "According to the pod's map, before we lost power, BridgeWater is north of Whisper Wood Valley, which I guess," he pointed to somewhere among the hills, "is over there."

"Everything's so real here," Kendall mused aloud. Unlike the steel and concrete jungles and artificial light they were used to, the world of the past shone with vibrancy and life. She couldn't help but stop and try to absorb as much of it as she could. She'd been waiting for the Dawn mission for ages, it seemed silly not to try and take in the very thing she'd come for.

Oliver and Eva ignored her remark. "If it's up there, we should get a move on," said Eva, a hand

perched above her eyes to shield them from the
sun.

"If Bridgewater's behind those hills, we've got
at least a few more days to go."

Oliver turned and squinted up toward the sun.
"We don't have much time before sunset."

Eva sighed and acquiesced, and they began
down the hill to search for a place to bed down
for the night. The thought of sleeping in the
wilderness, exposed and unprepared for any
predator or traveler that came upon them, was
more than daunting, but it won out over the
thought of spending yet more hours trekking
through dirt.

As they walked, Kendall allowed her mind to
wander back to their original directive. Should
they still try to collect samples? With no clear plan
to get themselves back to the Dawn and home,
there wasn't much more chance of getting seed
samples home. Not to mention, all of her sample
jars and vials were somewhere back on the Dawn,
probably shattered and floating through space.
She giggled to herself at the thought of walking
into Bridgewater, her pockets bristling with plant
cuttings and bundles of seeds. Oliver looked back
at her strangely, and she just shrugged and cleared
her throat, schooling her face back into a
reasonable expression.

"Does anyone know the date?" Oliver was far
behind them, sending little slides of dirt and rocks

down the hill with every other step. Each slip was accompanied by a muttered curse. "Fucking knew I shouldn't've come."

"The goal was mid-1850, but" she shook her head, "there was some tampering." That statement alone, accompanied by a grunting step down from a protruding tree root, held more emotion than Eva usually showed. Kendall knew she took the crash, the escape pod launches, the near deaths of most of the crew, deeply personally. Something had happened to the ship she guided so carefully through the cosmos, and it had let her down in its most critical moments.

"We knew this wouldn't be easy," Kendall said, "but we've made it this far. We're tired and hungry. It'll feel much better in the morning."

A few minutes later, trundling along much more even ground, Oliver spoke up again. "Well, we're basically halfway there now." He forced a chuckle.

"No turning back," said Kendall, voice heavy with meaning. Eva did nothing but lengthen her stride and the other two trotted to keep up.

"Let's just sleep here," said Oliver.

Eva sent a sharp look over her shoulder and didn't slow an inch. "I'm going to bet somebody heard thunder without lightning or saw great balls of fire streak toward the earth. People will come looking." They knew she was right, but the look

Oliver fixed to the back of Eva's head said he didn't want to.

The shadows lengthened, and the blue sky was replaced by a pink, then orange and red, and then the beginning shades of purple. Kendall's legs ached with every step, but she pushed forward, driven by her trust in Eva and the lack of anything else to do. Without a map they weren't sure where the CheckPoint Emerald Ranch was located but they knew it was just north of Bridgewater, so there was no point to bother Eva again.

Oliver had taken to muttering not quite to himself: "Up, up, up, up. Over. Down, down, down, down. Left, right, left, right. Over and under." His narration was somewhat of a comfort as another man-made thing in the forest, but the gap between the two of them and Eva widened further and further as she tried to get far enough away not to hear him.

They passed small ponds and bodies of water here and there, which Eva deemed safe to camp beside. She and Oliver fashioned spears and rudimentary basket traps, though Eva did most of the actual fish-catching to supplement their rations from the escape pods. They lit fires that burned only long enough to cook their catch, and then extinguished them and spent long hours sitting in the dark, listening to every rustle and crack and waiting to be ambushed.

The next night, Eva looked at her strangely, barely visible in the dark, and eventually burst out with, "We—we lost the others.

"They got separated at the pods, and when his lost power, we lost vitals from all the others. I thought I saw Terry's for a while, but anything could have happened." It seemed to take great effort to say it, as hauling something heavy up the side of a hill.

Kendall knew already. If they'd met others, they would have brought them, but there was no point searching in this near-endless wilderness. She nodded grimly and patted Eva's knee in a way she hoped was comforting. They could only hope the others had survived, and that they were safe and fed wherever they might be.

First watch often fell to Kendall, as the other two oversaw their meals. She stood, leaning against a tree or pacing around their sleeping bodies to keep herself awake, fighting off grief and exhausted tears. Sometimes, she did allow herself to cry, hand clasped over her mouth, pressed to a tree far enough away that she hoped they wouldn't hear her. These moments made it easier to trudge along during the day, meeting the others' despair with her own mostly-feigned optimism and support.

Her thoughts drifted often to her bed back home, both as she fought sleep and while they walked. She thought of her mother and the

routines she had instilled in Kendall, now lost to
the Dawn, somewhere high above her. She
wondered whether her family knew about the fate
of the Dawn, whether headquarters had gotten a
report of the incident, or if they sat at home,
waiting for the Dawn to reappear in their own
sky. Those nights she cried the hardest.
Day 18 of their journey proved to be particularly
grueling. They'd followed three different paths
that supposedly led north, but each path
ultimately brought them to a frustrating dead
end–the bank of a river, a sheer cliff wall, and the
edge of the forest itself. Twice they had had to
retrace their steps as best they could, frustration
rendering them unable to speak to one another in
more than clipped statements for hours or days.
On the third attempt, they fanned out, too angry
at themselves and each other to walk together,
and Oliver had discovered a thin wagon road in
the distance. He'd shouted so loudly and so
abruptly that Eva and Kendall tripped over
themselves to get to him, fearing he'd been
injured.

"We could take that path, there. I bet we'd be
in Bridgewater in a matter of days, rather than
wandering through all," he gestured at the
neverending sea of trees, "this."
Eva shook her head wearily. "You know we can't
do that." They'd already discussed the dangers of
roads and unprepared encounters. They were

faster, true, but some were patrolled, and people were naturally more skeptical of strangers they met in the wilds.

"Even in this area, we can't risk it," said Eva. "I won't let us risk it." Her voice firmed into something closer to what they'd heard on the Dawn.

Oliver put up his hands. "Alright, alright." They trudged back through the brush, feeling more of its weight as it tangled and pulled at their clothes and legs.

Kendall was of two minds. She wanted badly to be done with the discomfort and monotony of their walk, but she also wasn't one to introduce unpredictable variables. Meeting a person from this time felt like meeting an alien, and she wasn't quite sure she was ready for that.

It rained for the first time that night, and they quickened to a jog, fanning out to search for shelter as they ran. Oliver, their keenest observer, spotted it first: a cave nestled into the side of a hill beneath a towering, dangerously-leaning tree. He called them over, and the trio hurried toward the cave, relief rising and then disappearing just as quickly when they reached its mouth and saw it already occupied.

It was too late to turn back without being seen, and from what they could see, only one person sat beside a small fire, pushing the ash and logs around with a stick.

"Come on in!" he called. "There's room enough for everyone. That storm's gonna be nasty." His tone was welcoming, but Kendall held back behind the other two, keeping them between her and the man.

Inside, the stranger seemed neither threatening nor particularly interested in them. He politely offered cured sausage, bread, and cheese in what was likely an obligatory show of hospitality, as the first inhabitant of the cave, but then returned to his lounging, sipping at a flask of something he didn't offer. He offered no name, blankets, or bedroll, but didn't ask for any either.

"Thank you, thank you," Eva repeated over and over, and then, finding her courage, leaned over to ask, "Is it far to Bridgewater?" He thought for a moment, and then nodded slowly. "Mmm, about a day'f you take Pine Road." He pointed out into the rain in the direction of the cart road. Eva nodded and thanked him again, and the cave lapsed into silence save for the crackle of the fire and patter of the rain.

"Best be careful on the roads these days, though." The man seemed to have come to a conclusion, and abruptly broke the silence. "Them critter's 'r actin' funny. There's squids in the woods. Fire made of water. Birds'at never get tired. Strange men too, wandering about, lookin' for trouble."

The three expeditioners exchanged an uneasy look, each digesting the man's words in their own way, but deciding silently together what they should do. Kendall couldn't begin to decipher the words, but assumed they were some sort of metaphor like might be found in books or fairytales.

"Call themselves the Craftsmen. Now and then they take some poor bastard from town and nobody ever sees 'em again." He turned his head to look lazily between then. "You heard of 'em?"

"No, we haven't heard," Oliver responded, his voice nearing the edge of panic.

Eva took the opportunity to intervene. "Thank you, sir. We'll be sure to be careful. We should rest now, we have a long day ahead of us tomorrow." Her voice was light and lilting, not at all like she normally spoke.

The man nodded tiredly and tipped his hat over his eyes. "Just be careful out there. Those Craftsmen don't make their intentions easily seen, and you don't always know when someone's one of 'em." Then he shuffled himself into a more comfortable position and was promptly snoring away.

Kendall prepared to take her normal watch while Oliver and Eva curled up by the fire. She was grateful, in a way, that they'd travelled this long without knowing the full extent of the dangers in these woods, but she also knew the stranger's words for necessary so they could be prepared for what lay ahead of them.

When she went to wake Eva for her watch, she turned over before Kendall even laid a hand on her shoulder, and was stoking the fire before Kendall had taken her place on the cave floor. When she woke, the fire was nearly to ash and their companion was nowhere to be seen.

"Looks like he left a parting gift," Oliver said from the other side of the fire. In the place the man had been laying, they found a small pile of rolls and two links of sausage wrapped in a cloth. They each had a few bites of it and resolved to save the rest for their continued journey. Even that small meal felt like the best food Kendall had ever tasted, and she resolved never to take a hot meal for granted again.

They set out again, and the days continued to stack. Day 20 came, then day 23, and Kendall felt as if she had been doing nothing but walking forever. Her old life and the technological comforts of home and the Dawn were a distant memory which the exhaustion and hunger sometimes made it hard to remember, and still they trudged on, determined that over each new rise, Bridgewater would appear below them and their journey would finally be over.

Terry.
18??

Confusion was his first sensation. Then a rush of panic. He remembered alarms blaring, and then silence. He opened his eyes and the world spun around him, colors blending together like watercolor. He blinked and shook his head again and again, and then hauled himself out of his splintered pod and the gash of mud and pebbles it had carved in the earth. Still, it was hard to stand, but the cooling sensation of the earth, and getting himself to a half-standing position helped to slow the spinning.

The only landmark he recognized was the mountain, high in the distance among a range of shorter peaks, but his own thoughts ran like mice through his head, disappearing around corners before he could grasp their tails. The mountain was important—the tallest one, with snow in its cap. Forest beneath it. All he could hear was the ringing in his own ears.

He took one step at a time, pausing between each to pant and fight the nausea, leaning heavily on trees to keep himself upright.

Where was the door? He had to stay calm. Around here somewhere? He had to get to it.

He'd lost sight of the mountain beneath the canopy of leaves. Surely, he was headed toward it. He had nowhere else to go, but squinting to force the world into stillness only revealed endless forest and his pod, cracked like an egg, half-buried behind him.

Wherever the others were, he hoped they had fared better, that their pods had safer landings and they were finding each other and regrouping. They would go on with the mission. He would go to the mountain.

Belly of the mount—his head swam with flashing lights, keyboards of strange symbols, wires, faces stern and smiling. In emergency, open the door. Find the Bridge.
He could feel the pull of it, deep in his gut, now that the nausea had calmed. He knew he was going the right way. Even as darkness began to fall and fatigue dragged at him, he continued one foot in front of the other, even dragging them through the dry leaves on the ground, only stopping to catch his breath and stare up through the trees for any glimpse of the white cap of the mountain.

He would walk through the night if he had to. For as many nights as it took.

Oliver
18??

Off in the distance, a small town shimmered in the evening light. Oliver felt his spirits soar, knowing he was letting them get too high. Civilization meant safety, but no more chance of recovering the dawn or returning to their own time and families. Still, he let it wash over him and keep his weary legs going.

They found only a few buildings, most of them homes or stores, and a post office. An eerie stillness was blanketed over the place. Plenty of lights were on, even a few in the windows, but no smoke rose from the chimneys and no people or animals walked the streets. They spread into a single line across the road as they walked, almost by instinct, taking in their surroundings and walking in near lockstep.

On the other end of the town's single main road, they found a single-story inn and clustered on the side of the road a few yards from its entrance, deliberating.

"New Haven." Oliver said. Kendall gave him a searching look, and he pointed to a cracking wooden sign out front. The words New Haven Inn could barely be seen painted across it.

They both looked to Eva, accustomed to her guidance.

"Contact without proper preparation is more dangerous than camping."

"Camping?" Kendall piped up. "I think we've camped more than enough. All the protocols are shot to hell. We may as well be warm." Eva glared at Kendall but didn't say anything to argue. Tensions between the three of them had risen steadily throughout their walk, culminating in a frustrated silence and now an impasse. Oliver had long decided he would rather risk Eva's wrath than spend another night on the ground.

"Isn't this what we were looking for?" Eva turned her glare on Oliver and Kendall threw a hand up in agreement. Oliver shrugged and met Eva's eyes. "I'm sleeping in a bed tonight."

"Fine!" Eva abruptly turned and started toward the inn's door without looking back. Oliver almost felt bad, but one look out into the ink-black distance quelled any of that. He and Kendall fell into silent step behind Eva.

Eva was setting her first foot under the front eaves of the inn when the creak and movement of a closing window caught all of their attention a few rooms down. When she reached out to the handle of the front door, the crack of a slamming door echoed through the dark, and she startled and stepped back, colliding with Oliver and nearly knocking him into Kendall. He ducked to the side and helped Eva to steady herself. She kept stepping backward until she was alongside Kendall, her face pale as a sheet and her hands obviously shaking, more afraid than Oliver thought she was capable of. He opened his mouth to ask her what was wrong and caught nearly the same expression on Kendall's face, her eyes shiny and wide.

"What–" Then he realized they weren't staring at his face but somewhere over his shoulder, and Eva's hand had come up to grip vise-like at Kendall's elbow.

Turning back to the door, Oliver found himself staring down the barrel of a gun. It was strange seeing one in person, so close to his face he could smell spent gunpowder and the oil probably used to clean it. They'd read about these prehistoric weapons in training, practiced holding them, firing pretend plastic mock-ups, disarming an attacker, but there was something different about seeing one in metal. Absurdly, what struck him first was that all their practice had been on weapons almost comically inflated and badly-proportioned, and that the proportions of the one he saw looked much more comfortable to hold and fire.

Behind the gun, once he'd unstuck himself from marveling at it, stood a boy no older than sixteen, his eyes wide and determined. Oliver got his breath under control and slowly began raising open palms on either side of his head.

"We mean no harm," came Eva's voice. "And we have—" there was some fumbling that made the boy twitch the gun toward her, then back to Oliver. "We have money. To pay."

The boy scanned each of them, eyes lingering at their waists and ankles, clearly checking for concealed weapons. Oliver had lost his in the chaos on the Dawn and was grateful for it now. He stood as still as he could, breathing deeply, willing his face to be soft and unthreatening.

Eventually, the barrel of the gun dipped slightly and the boy edged to the side to get a better look at Eva and Kendall. Oliver didn't dare turn and could only hope they had followed his lead.

"Fine. C'mon in." The boy let the barrel point toward the floor but didn't take either hand off of it, then stepped back and gestured with his head for them to follow.

The entire building was wooden from the floors to the ceiling, the counter, all the chairs, even the windowsills and casings. Oliver saw Kendall's giddy expression out of the corner of his eye and had to agree. This was a dream come true, if not exactly the circumstances he would have wanted.

There was a rich, heady aroma of smoke and wood, a far cry from the sterile, recycled air of the Dawn. There were a few lanterns along the walls, and each cast a warm, flickering light. Not a single blue, green, or red light in sight. No blinking monitors. No whirring life support machinery in the background. Every creak of the floorboards, puff of cigarette smoke out of the clerk's mouth, crackle from the fireplace felt like a revelation. "Come on," Oliver felt Kendall pull at his elbow and realized Eva was already seated at an open table. He made his way haltingly over to sit down.

A minute or two passed where they continued to marvel together at the room and the few other patrons, shifting uncomfortably in their own woefully conspicuous clothing. In hindsight, no wonder the boy had been suspicious. Another pang of regret went through Oliver. He was glad they'd come in, but regretted not listening more closely to Eva's concerns.

Another door slammed, but no one in the room seemed phased. To the right of the counter, a man with a beer belly and a cloth tied around his head emerged from a door that bounced off of the wall beside it with a crash and fell closed again. The man lumbered over to their table and gestured at each of them unceremoniously.

"Three. Bread?" He waited barely a few seconds while the three of them looked frantically between each other, then smirked and leaned over

Oliver. "Probably best," he chuckled lowly. "I wouldn't want to waste my time with Sally's," he hooked a thumb over his shoulder at a ruffly woman lounging at a corner table, "stale buns."

Oliver sat stock-still, stunned and utterly confused, while the room filled with scattered laughter. Another man sitting close to Sally punched his overly-amused neighbor in the shoulder, and they both began bickering in hushed voices. Sally rolled her eyes and turned her back to Oliver's table.

The man didn't wait for any of them to reply and instead disappeared back through the door, chuckling to himself. "Three! Bread!" he called to someone out of sight.

From there, the room went back to a companionable, low drone. The other patrons occasionally shot unreadable glances at the newcomers' table, but no one moved to bother them.

A different man came over to their table to deliver bread and bowls of an unidentifiable soup. "You'll be needing rooms?" He looked over the three of them quizzically.

Eva spoke up, "Two please." He nodded slowly but didn't move.

"You three from the city?" They all nodded, smiles now plastered to their faces. "Best be careful passin' through here. Don't want to get on the wrong side of the Gems." He surveyed their faces and continued when they didn't show signs of recognition. "From the Ranch, other side of the mountain. Boy over there," he jerked his head in the direction of the boy with the shotgun, who was now loitering around the kitchen door, "lost his mother to the Gems. 'S why he's so jumpy. Can't be too careful these days." He stood there for another quiet moment before Eva shook herself and went to fumble a few coins out of her bag. They glinted silver as she slid them across the table. He picked them up, turned them over a few times, then glanced between their faces, making a soft humming noise.

"How many nights you all be needin' the rooms?"

"Just one." Oliver had the distinct feeling of wanting to flee out the door.

The innkeeper nodded again and deliberately placed two of the coins back on the table with a click. "Last two on the row. You jus' go out the door you came and take a left. Go to the counter for the keys first."

They all nodded again and the innkeeper finally sidled away, disappearing through the kitchen door.

The three of them settled down to eat, discovering that the bread was warm, if a little stale, and the soup hearty and tasty. A flag caught Oliver's eye over the front door. It had been painted directly onto the wood of the wall, and though he recognized the colors and pattern of the American flag, a deep green border covered in strange symbols gave him pause. That had never been mentioned in their training. He could only wonder what it meant. Squinting at it, the symbols looked hand painted and clumsy, as if drawn by a child. He wondered if the boy with the gun had drawn them.

A man stood from a table across the room, toting a huge mug of beer, and sidled over to their table, sitting in the only open chair without stopping to ask permission. He cast a feeling of unspoken intention over the table, and once he'd made himself comfortable, took a folded piece of paper from his pocket, unfolded it carefully, and laid it out across the table in front of a jittery Oliver. He then stabbed a finger onto a line across the paper and began to speak.

"I'd stay well clear of the main roads, I were you." He slid his finger along the map. "It gets worse than you'd think, over here." Eva stiffened almost imperceptibly next to the man. Kendall looked as if she'd rather slept on a rock pile than this. Oliver was starting to agree.

"You go over there on your own time." He leaned closer to Oliver and his deep, twanging accent abrupty disappeared. "I'd hit the train station." He tapped its location on the map. Oliver wondered if he was somehow supposed to understand what this man was saying. He racked his brain, searching for any measure of recognition, and found absolutely nothing.

"Head toward the big hill to the north." His finger slid and tapped. "Stay off the main roads, shelter under the trees. Isn't too cold for that yet. You'll be fine." He pinned each of them with a pointed gaze. "I wouldn't want to go, mine you, but needs must." He straightened a bit and looked between each of them again.

"Not to judge, but I see two women and one man. There more of ya?" The accent had returned. Oliver shook his head hesitantly and Eva fixed him with the most controlled furious gaze he'd seen yet. Kendall was avoiding eye contact altogether, scraping at the bottom of her bowl with her spoon.
"You'll never make it to Emerald Ranch," the man declared bluntly, plainly frustrated by their confusion. He shook his head, swept up and re-folded the map, and scraped the feet of his chair across the floor as he stood.

"Up, come on." When none of them moved, he flapped the map at them and gestured to the door. "You don't want to walk the whole way, do you?" That raised Oliver's interest, and he stood to follow the man even as Kendall and Eva took several more seconds to reluctantly trail behind.

The man took them to the other side of the inn, where there was a stable and a few stalls full of snuffling horses.

"Five of 'em," said the man. "All yours tomorrow. Get somebody inside to help you saddle 'em. Then don't use those coins anymore. Looks suspicious."

"How did you come by these horses?" Eva finally piped up, she and Kendall lingering by the stable's wide doorway, leaving themselves an easy escape route.

The man shrugged. "Picked 'em up here and there. Doesn't matter. They won't cause you any trouble." To Oliver's admittedly untrained eye, all the horses looked alert and well cared-for. It vaguely occurred to him that none of them had ever ridden before, but as this strange man had said: "Needs must."

"There's some hard tack and jerky in the saddlebags and a few bedrolls." He stopped and considered silently for a moment. "You sure you don't want to keep at it tonight? They're pretty suspicious of you in there." Eva nodded firmly and stepped further into the stable.

"He's right. We can get a few hours from here and then rest." This time, neither of them argued with her, and they spent the next several minutes watching the mysterious man saddle and bridle the horses, then lead them one-by-one out into the yard and helped them mount. As they passed under the frame of the stable door, Oliver saw more symbols carved into the wood all around it.

They looked like the ones around the flag, but steadier and worn smooth.

"River's thataway." He pointed. "Few miles down, you'll find another village. The road splits there. If you turn south, you'll come to a little white house with a, well, it's—"

"Ethos Watchtower," said Eva. Oliver and Kendall looked at her in surprise.

The man's expression faltered slightly, something like suspicion flashing across his face, but he quickly recovered and charged on. "That's right. Just be careful over there. There can be a few…unpredictables."

He checked the horses over one more time, cursorily explained how to direct them, gave each an approving nod, and pointed again in the direction they should go. "Few miles, turn south, keep an eye peeled. Stay off the main roads, whatever you do." Then he tapped each horse's haunch, and off they walked into the darkness, the horses falling into step behind one-another.

When they looked back, just before they turned a corner and lost sight of the inn altogether, the boy, the innkeeper, and a few others lined the open doorway and the windows, watching them go. It made the hairs on Oliver's arms stand up, and he, Kendall, and Eva urged their horses faster, bouncing unsteadily along toward the river.

It was a clear night, the stars bright and clear above them. To occupy himself, Oliver focused on relaxing into the horse's gait and trying to recall the shapes of the symbols he'd seen at the inn. They gnawed at him, unsettling in their unfamiliarity, but he felt strongly that he'd regret it later if he let himself forget.

Eva rode point, vigilant as ever and keeping their pace as fast as she could get her horse to go without falling off. The air was full of the sounds of nocturnal animals, and that was simultaneously a new wonder of this ancient world and an unsettling reminder of their lack of place within it. Oliver tried not to dwell too much on that, directing his thoughts back to those symbols, their curves and angles, and adjusted his grip on the reins. The shock of their brief time at the inn was beginning to wear off, and he could already tell he would be falling asleep in his seat before long. He hoped they would stop soon, but not before they got plenty of distance between themselves and the strange town of New Haven.

Lewis
1861

The group that now surrounded them was rag-tag, mismatched, but they moved with a level of comfort and fluidity that only comes with deep familiarity and trust. Lewis' eyes darted from one to the next, taking in their appearances, trying to piece together who might be friendly or hostile.

The archer was easy to spot. He was a small, thin man, younger than many of the rest with a curly mop of hair bouncing atop his head. He carried the bow with casual ease, the strap of his quiver swinging loosely in his grip. Beside him all the time was a goliath–at least two heads above the archer, with arms like tree trunks. He carried a coiled whip at his belt, but it shone with a strange iridescence in the moonlight.

They both were speckled with dark spots–mud or blood–that Lewis found himself equally curious and horrified over. Mud was expected. They were in the forest, after all, but blood–Lewis resolved to stay clear of them both.

The third was wiry like the first, but carried a pack so large it threatened to overwhelm him. The straps and loops on the outside carried all manner of knives, loops of rope, even a small woodsman's axe, and dispersed among those were trinkets and baubles that Lewis couldn't begin to identify, all carrying that same sheen as the large man's whip.

The group moved with purpose, all three of their heads on a continuous swivel, surveying the trees and shadows between them. There was a tension in the air fueled by the three men's silence and the strange looks they gave each other and Sam and Lewis as they took turns rifling through the wagon. Lewis' heart pounded in his chest, threatening to burst at any sudden movement.

That pounding and anxiety had begun to feel familiar in a way Lewis didn't like. It seemed that the second he and Sam got through one peril, another came right on its heels. What he wouldn't give for a soft bed and some warm food.

"Hey, boy, put away that knife. Yer makin' me nervous. Plus, by man over there would cut your neck three different ways before you got one." The big man with the whip called, not apparently concerned about being heard.

"I doubt it," Sam's voice was lower and angrier than Lewis had ever heard it, "and I ain't no boy." He spit the last word and made no move to sheath the sharp bit of stone he'd picked up when they were captured.

"So you aren't." The man made a clumsy mock salute. "My fault, boss, yeah."

"Go on, get back up in your trees and leave us alone. Make as much noise leaving as you did getting here, so we know where you are."

"You hear that, Arlyn? He thinks we make too much noise! As if you'd ever hear us if we didn't mean you to." He knelt down just out of Sam's reach and spread his hands in supplication. "Come on now. Throw that stone away and and we'll put some food in that rumbling tummy of yours, hey? We don't mean you any harm." Sam stared resolutely back, making no move to comply.

The big man shrugged. "You're in BrownCreek territory. Wouldn't want one of them crackers to find you. No place for men such as yourself to be wandering alone."

"He's not alone." Lewis tried for his most intimidating voice, but the smile that met him said he hadn't succeeded.

"So there's two of you. No matter. Listen here, son," he turned back to Sam, "numbers don't mean much if you don't know how to use 'em." His eyes flicked back to the man with the huge pack, standing as if it weighed nothing, who had emerged from the back of the wagon and gave a thumbs-down.

"You think you're tough, huh? Well, you ain't. Out here, toughness means surviving. It's knowing when to fight, he stood and his voice hardened pointedly, "and when to back down. You boys don't look like you know either." Lewis glanced at Sam and saw resignation begin to dawn.

"We're not looking for trouble," Lewis said, silently urging Sam to hasten his decision. "We just want to move on."

"Move on, huh? Well, why don't you move on with us? We can keep you safe, might even learn a thing or two." The archer, clearly bored of the conversation, was drifting back and forth between the trees, scanning the darkness without much sense of urgency.

"'S a nice horse." Arlyn piped up after a moment. "Where'd you steal 'em from?"

"We didn't steal anything." Sam gritted his teeth. The big man made a placating gesture and shot a disapproving look at Arlyn.

"Would you at least tell us your names?" Lewis said. The tension was beginning to give him a headache.

"I'm Kyro," said the big man with the whip. "Ugly one over there's Arlyn," he gestured to the bowman.

"Hey, fuck you," Arlyn called back through the trees.

"Other one's Rufio. Now yours."

"Sam. Lewis." Sam pointed to each of them.

"We're Scarabs," said Lewis, which prompted shocked laughter from the other men.

"No you're not," said Arlyn, plainly disgusted. Lewis looked between them, bewildered.

"I think they mean they were going to be scarabs," said Kyro, looking to them for confirmation. "People don't escape from Emerald Ranch."

"Explains the wagon, and the chains." Rufio gestured to the back of the wagon. "What'd you do to 'em?"

"Doesn't matter," said Kyro before either of them could reply. He extended a hand and Sam reluctantly dropped the stone in favor of taking it and being hauled to his feet. Then Kyro came over to Lewis and helped him up too.

"Who are you?" asked Lewis. "Why're d'you want to help us?"

Kyro shrugged. "We're free men," he said simply.

"You ready to get moving? Not injured?" Sam and Lewis shook their heads, and Kyro gestured for them to start walking through the deepening shadows. Arlyn walked far ahead of them and Rufio behind a little ways, leading the horse.

"How far?" asked Lewis. Sam looked as if he wished he had used the knife on Lewis and walked as far from Kyro as he could.

"It's a long ways northeast, but we'll get there easy enough. We'll stop at a house nearby, first. Got some friends who work there. We'll get you some hot food. Enjoy it, we'll rough it the rest of the way."

"What do you mean 'friends'," Sam said.

"Friends," Kyro deadpanned. "You forgotten what friends are?"

Sam pointedly ignored that. "You better not be getting any wise ideas."

"Relax. We'll trade the horse for some supplies. You know, the one you stole. Think of it as thanks for our help.

An arrow whizzed by Kyro's ear and embedded itself a ways up a tree behind them. Kyro didn't even flinch. Lewis looked past him to see Arlyn, bow already slung across his back and heading to scale the tree. Sam and Lewis stood stock-still as he clambered up and dropped down a moment later with a writhing handful of squirrel. He held it up to Kyro. "See, same here."

Kyro gestured for Sam and Lewis to come closer, then indicated the movement of the squirrels limbs, still flinging as if running or swimming. The arrow had gone through the back of its head, and its neck held on by a bare thread. "We're gonna eat that?" Lewis said.

"You're a fool if you do," Rufio said from behind them. "You don't eat something if it don't go where you send it first." His wording struck Lewis as odd, and Sam looked at him in open confusion.

"The animals 'round here, they ain't right. Don't die like they're supposed to. See how it's still moving? Something's got ahold of it, like it don't know it's dead. You eat something like that, you might not know when you're dead," said Kyro.

"The deer do the same," said Arlyn. "You shoot 'em and they take off running, trip over their own feet and just lay there, kicking their legs, arrow straight through their heart."

"Birds fall from the sky without anything touching 'em, flap around like they're still up there," said Rufio.

Sam had gone pale. "Alright, we'll go with you. No funny business."

Kyro put up his hands, and his two compatriots both rolled their eyes. "No funny business. No problem. Let's keep moving." Arlyn shoved the still-thrashing squirrel into a pouch which he slung over his shoulder. The pouch twitched and made scratching noises as the squirrel scrabbled mindlessly against it. Lewis suppressed a gag.

They walked parallel to the mud-splattered road for a while, the horse snorting and sidestepping at shadows behind them. Before long, Lewis and Sam found themselves talking almost openly with the strange men, who seemed eager to chat about themselves as well as ask friendlier questions about Sam and Lewis.

"Quiet from here," Kyro said after a while, and they all fell silent together.

The landscape shifted as they trekked, and a dilapidated farmhouse came into view. On their way toward it. The twang of another arrow came from Arlyn's direction, and a bird fell into the crown of a nearby tree. Arlyn and Rufio exchanged and look, and then Rufio rolled his eyes, handed the horse off to Kyro, and went none-to-gracefully up the tree. They all stood around in silence, waiting.

"You think these two'll be enough?" Kyro asked Arlyn, who shrugged.

"If not, it'll be close. He can get the others himself."

When Rufio returned with a fresh-scraped elbow and the still-flapping body of a duck, they set off again, drawing ever closer to the farmhouse. Lewis and Sam exchanged a glance and nod, following the other three through the door once they'd tied the horse.

"Welcome to our little sanctuary," Kyro flung out his arms in exaggerated welcome, indicating the space inside.

The walls were lined with all manner of things Lewis couldn't identify. Tools, scraps of cloth, and boxes of every size imaginable. It was dimly lit with a few dying lanterns, and Kyro shook his head at them. "Dammit, man. Got to keep them oiled."

A tall, muscular man with scars up and down his arms emerged from a doorway. "You were supposed to be here hours ago," he barked."

"Here: duck and a squirrel." Kyro gestured for Arlyn to hand them over, and the man snatched the pouch away and eagerly yanked it open.

"This don't make up for it." Then he turned to shout back through the doorway. "They're back!"

Another man emerged, this one slightly older with glasses and a bloodstained apron. He rubbed his eyes as if newly awakened. "I'm coming, I'm coming. S'posed to be here hours ago, now we're all urgent." The tall man immediately handed him the still-moving bag, and the old man peered excitedly inside.

"Same place as last time?" Kyro and Arlyn nodded grimly.

"Don't just stand there," the scarred man snapped, gesturing to a table and chairs. "You two, go sit down."

They sat, but Lewis' eyes and head kept moving, trying to take in the myriad of strange objects lining the walls. Every time he glanced back over a section, he noticed something new. Curiosity had long overridden any mistrust he felt, but he still felt tension radiating from Sam beside him.

After a moment, the scarred man joined them, Kyro and Arlyn disappearing into another room and Rufio disappearing outside to tend the horse.

"So, you were gonna be Scarabs, huh?" Lewis nodded slowly. "Lucky you. Folks go in there, they don't come out."

"We're looking for somewhere safe," said Lewis.

"Safe, huh? Well, you might find that here for a bit, but safety's a tricky thing 'round here."

Kyro and Arlyn re-emerged with hot food, rolls, and water, which they distributed to everyone and then pulled chairs up to sit with them. They ate in silence for a long time, and then impatience got the better of Sam and he spoke up.

"When can we go?"

The scarred man didn't look up from his plate. "Not tonight, not out there. We're not really in the business of sending people to their deaths.

"Can't go north—that's nothing but mountain. You head east, you'll run right back to where you came from. Go south, right to Emerald Ranch. There are other plantations here and there—mind you, not like the one y'all ran from."

"Never you mind about that though," Kyro interjected. You're not alone in this. We're gonna get you somewhere safe."

"Here's to bad information," Rufio said, throwing back a shot of dark liquor. The man with the bloodstained apron reappeared through a doorway. "Not my fault you three can't find the right people. They're obviously not Gems." He gestured to Sam and Lewis.

"It wasn't bad info. Muriel gave me those coordinates, and I gave them to you," said the scarred man.

"And we went in that direction, and they weren't there," Rufio insisted.

"You sure you could see straight? You're awfully friendly with that bottle?" said the man in the apron.

"You had bad info. Wasn't your fault, but we still wasted a day or more." Kyro, unamused by the scolding, raised a hand between them. "Makes no matter. We need to find those three and then head out. We need the power."

"Power?" Lewis muttered, tearing off another hunk of bread.

Rufio, smirking at Lewis, dug through his backpack and pulled out a silver square, which he placed gingerly on the table and a piece of fabric next to it. Then, he dug out a scrap of leather and laid it over an apple he'd been eating. Holding the fabric in one hand and the square of silver in the other, he hovered them above the apple on either side, then brought them firmly down. There was a faint shimmering line between the square and the fabric, almost like spiderweb, and the there was a bit of resistance when it met the leather, and then it passed cleanly through it and the apple.

"The history of mankind has been one of unrelenting forward progress," intoned Kyro over the presentation. "So much technology today boggles the imagination, and the Gems and command so much of it.

"This string is thin enough to be almost invisible," the men at the table smiled knowingly, "but strong enough to be almost unbreakable." The apple fell into two clean halves, dark seeds stark against the white flesh. Barely a drop of juice darkened the table.

Kendall.
18??

Kendall fought to suppress the rising tide of anxiety within her. She couldn't shake the foreboding sense of danger that cloaked herself and the path ahead.

"But we were warned to stay off the road!" Oliver's protest rang out, stark against the hum of nightime noise.

"He was far too sure of our route. Like I said, this is my second time here. These places are notorious for gangs and thieves. He could just as easily have sent us directly into a trap.

Kendall shivered. Her mind filled with images of ambushes and hidden dangers. The forest pressed in, once fascinating in its abundance and life, now sinister. Every rustle of leaves, every creak of branches set her nerves alight. Eva, resolute and unyielding, was her only comfort.

"I guess." It was clear that hadn't crossed Oliver's mind.

"There was more shit in that stable than these few horses could produce. He likely sent his friends ahead and pointed us right to them. No telling what could happen to us." Eva had led them to the east, once they got out of sight of the inn, immediately locating the road and starting them along it. They rode for longer than any of them wanted, but a prevailing anxiety kept either Oliver or Kendall from arguing with Eva about it.

They rode nearly half the night before she deemed it safe to stop. With every blink, Kendall felt herself slip a little off the saddle and had to right herself every few minutes. Oliver leaned heavily over his horse's neck. Eva led them a ways off the road, tied all three of their horses to a tree, and gave them water from a saddlebag. She insisted they have no fire, which set Oliver to grumbling and roughly flinging his bedroll open. No fire meant no hot food and nothing else to do but sleep, so they spent a few minutes sullenly eating hard tack and jerky before curling up in their bedrolls.

The night continued strangely peacefully. A half-moon peeked through the trees, surrounded by stars. Kendall sighed and settled in, feeling a bittersweet sense of awe. She couldn't imagine the vast breadth of time and progress that had taken the Earth from this to their own time, which were so different from each other as to be alien altogether.

"I'll take first watch," said Eva, startling Kendall. She hadn't considered watches.

She didn't have to wait long before sleep claimed her, and then Oliver was shaking her awake and announcing her turn to watch.

She had to stand and pace beside the bedrolls, bored and barely awake, but for the hours of her watch no one disturbed them, and then the sun was rising and the other two were sitting up and rubbing sleep out of their eyes. They gathered their things, lashed them inexpertly to the horses' saddles, gave the horses more water, and mounted back up.

Progress that day was maddeningly slow. Eva navigated them by memory, sometimes having to double back or sweep wide for landmarks she recognized. Neither Kendall nor Oliver knew where they were going anymore, but they followed without complaint.

"Smoke!" Eva eventually declared, pointing over the trees.

Northward, still a long ways away, a curling column of smoke stood proudly against the blue sky. They came over a ridge, and there were the smoking remains of a cluster of buildings, which stopped them firmly for a moment, Eva going quiet and stern. They came upon a pair of bodies in a tree, swaying in the wind.

"Runaway slaves, no doubt," muttered Oliver. The crows had just begun to peck at them, but they scattered when the horses approached.

"We should let them down," Kendall said thickly.

"No!" commanded Eva, spurring them into movement again. "This is not our place or time. We stay out of it. Remember your mission." Kendall had never seen a corpse before, but in stories they always swarmed with clouds of flies. These, though, were bare and quiet, with only the crows slowly returning to pick at them.

"If that's the town I think it is," Eva made a frustrated sound and paused, "Nimblepine and Emerald Ranch are a few miles beyond it. We'll keep to the outskirts."

Trailing well around the burned town, they passed over a stream and stopped to let the horses drink and take a few mouthfuls of grass. Kendall, hot and sore from riding, slipped off, knelt on a wide, flat rock, and plunged her face into the water, squealing as she came up again. Oliver was in the middle of following her when Eva barked at them. "Hey! Get up, quick, we have company." Her eyes were wide and fearful, and Oliver and Kendall scrambled to obey. The horses, enjoying the water and grass, were reluctant to obey their urging, and Eva eventually circled back around them to smack sharply at their backsides. Both horses leapt away through the trees, Kendall barely able to hold on.

Together, they hurtled over ditches and logs, a cohort of men in black garb appearing behind them on horses of their own. Hooves thundered. Kendall's focus narrowed to keeping herself astride her horse, allowing it to choose its own frantic course through the trees. Dogs barked and snarled behind them.

"Eva?" Oliver called.

"We had half a day's start on them." Eva's voice jittered with the impact of her horse's hooves. "They've been chasing us since midday."

"We ought to be able to take a few of them," Oliver called, his voice pained.

"It's at least three to one!" Kendall shrieked. They were gaining.
The chase drove them toward a small lake, the horses beginning to pant and flag. It began to dawn on Kendall that they were going to be caught and left to the mercy of these strange, frightening men.

"Drop your weapons! We ain't gonna hurt ya!" A voice called from behind them, far too close for comfort. A single man emerged from the pack, hefting a longbow over his horse's shoulder. An arrow barely missed Kendall's left elbow. Something told her it was a warning shot.

Eva's face was a mask of stony determination as she pulled up behind Kendall. "Stay ahead! Zigzag best you can."

They came upon a wall of trees that Kendall swore were swaying without any wind. As they passed through it, there was a yell and a crash behind them as a rider was knocked off his mount. Then another as a man was yanked bodily up into the branches of another tree. There was a sharp movement over Kendall's shoulder, and she felt herself being hurtled through the air, her horse up on its hind legs, then skittering sideways and away through the trees. She lay there, gasping for breath, hearing screams and the thudding of terrified hooves.

"Ken!" She sat up to see Oliver standing up a few yards away, the reins of his panicking horse clutched firmly in one hand. He hefted a stone and flung it at a man advancing on Kendall. The stone struck him and clattered to the ground, making no impact, and the man kept coming. Eva hurled something shiny from a tree much farther away, and Kendall had just enough time to register what it was before the world went white and spiderwebbed. Fresh screams erupted around her, and Kendall curled into herself against the pain of the sudden light.

She felt herself being lifted and fought against her captor, trying to pry his hands from her waist and arms.

"Hey, it's me!" came Oliver's voice, and she was hefted up onto a warm back. She felt him climb up after her, and she clutched at him as he urged the horse forward again.

"Wish I had my gun!" Oliver shouted.

"I want none of your words right now, science man," Eva bellowed. She was ahead of them now, but Kendall's vision still flickered and blurred too much to see. "Small changes—" she huffed a labored breath, "to the time-timeline as we know it—unpredictable variations to-to the f-future."

"So we let them kill us?" Oliver's voice was high and strained. The horse pulled to an abrupt stop, and Oliver helped Kendall off the horse, urged it to run away, and then he and Eva helped Kendall to climb a rocky slope and then duck behind a jutting boulder, where they slumped into a crevice, their knees pressed uncomfortably to one-another. Rain began to wet their heads and shoulders.

"For a moment," Eva panted. "Then we move on."

Simmons
1872

Simmons leaned heavily against the corner wall, desperately trying to catch his breath and perched in the shadows, the scent of spilled liquor and discharged gunpowder hanging in the air. He looked down at the scattered spent bullet casings and wished he'd gotten here sooner.

"Fuckin' dramatic," he muttered and shared a look with Steve, adjusting his grip on his own revolver.

Movement flashed outside the windows—men taking their positions along the train.

"Hold them off!" Steve shouted, shattering a window with his first shot. He readjusted and shot again, ducking and popping back up as the Pinkertons shot back. Jimmy took another window, but Sherane slid down to sit on the floor against a chair, massaging her temples.

Simmons shuffled over to take Steve's place while he crouched to reload. His revolver was a lethal blend of intricate craftsmanship and cutting-edge technology. The barrel was long and reinforced with brass. Small, intricate gears and cogs adorned the barrel, whirring and ticking so his thumb never touched the hammer, but the gun kept smoothly firing shot after shot.

Simmons had asked once what made the smoke of each shot blue rather than the normal black, but Steve just smiled and said someone had "owed him a favor," and wouldn't say any more about it.

"There's too many of 'em. We ain't prepared for this!" The way Steve grimly finished reloading and took his place at the next window told Simmons he agreed. They'd prepared for some gunplay to subdue the passengers, maybe take out any overly-brave guards, but not a full-blown battle. The thought of the collateral alone made him shudder.

"Retreat, regroup!" Simmons' gun clicked empty and he ducked and crawled with difficulty toward the forward door. He saw Sherane finally take her head out of her hands and reach to pick up a discarded gun, flipping the barrel open to check for ammo before tucking it into a pocket and following him. As he passed the desk the two train owners had been hiding behind, he saw only open air and a square of missing floorboards wide enough for a person to squeeze through.

"They're—" he rose to a crouched run and went to stare down into the dark below the floor. "They're gone!" He reached into the hole and cast around but found nothing. The side of his head pressed against the floor, he instead caught a glimpse of pale, rough wood under a black blanket shoved under the desk. He wouldn't have seen it at all, entirely in shadow and behind the chair, but the gust of wind that blew through when Sherane opened the door to the engine ruffled the fabric just enough to expose a sliver of wood. He abandoned the hole in the floor to knock the chair out of the way with his shoulder and yanked the blanket off, exposing an unmarked wooden crate.

That had to be it. Just as Steve had said. But why wasn't it with the others? He was in the middle of trying to stand and heft the crate into the light when a hand clamped over his shoulder and yanked him back and down. He stumbled and twisted, falling to hands and knees as bullets zipped over his head.

"We can't hold 'em! We gotta go!" It was Kenny, who must have come back through from the engine when no one followed Sherane. The door flapped and clanged against its frame as bullets hit it and ricocheted.

"Come on!" Steve held the door open and he and Jimmy took turns laying covering fire while the others and then themselves darted onto the engine's rear platform.

She pushed the door open and darted across the coupling to the platform of the engine, and then set about gathering themselves up the narrow stairs and into the engine room. But a foot wedged itself into the door right before it closed, and then the face and body of a Pinkerton followed it, with others behind him, emerging from the car they had just left.

Sherane's shoulders gave a twitch, as if she were going to raise her twin guns again, but stilled again when she saw the mass of them crowding the doorway, the platform, the base of the stairs. Simmons, the last to mount the stairs and the closest to the Pinkertons, backpedaled up the steps, nearly tripping himself and Steve right behind him.

"Hey, don't fucking move!" yelled the closest Pinkerton. He wore a fine black coat over a vest and white shirt. Rings flashed on his fingers. His shoes were pristine and shined to a near-mirror finish, certainly not the shoes of a working man of the law.

Now that he could look at them, all of the guns currently trained on himself and his associates were held by finely dressed patrons of the Dice. Men and women alike, dressed in the finery of the recklessly wealthy, lined every inch of his vision. He even saw a badge on the chest of one, exposed by a discarded coat. He silently cursed himself and each and every one of his associates.

"Disguises," he heard Steve mutter at his back, "clever."

"The bomb." Jimmy, from somewhere above, called over the crowd. Simmons saw a ripple go through the Pinkertons.
"You! Shut up!" the closest Pinkerton stepped forward, gesturing his gun at Simmons and Steve. "What bomb?"

Simmons felt Steve's hand on his shoulder, then saw his hands begin to raise out of the corner of his eye. "How much time?"

"It could go off any–" and then the sky caught fire.

Oliver.
18??

They headed out as soon as the weather allowed and Kendall got her feet back under her. It wasn't long after they departed, easily finding their bearings, that they spotted more smoke. Two thin trails this time, headed toward the clouds.

"Hopefully only fireplaces," Oliver remarked, squinting into the distance.

"Should be Nimblepine," said Eva.

"A nice warm bed, food," Oliver rambled on, detailing all the things he was looking forward to in civilization.

But Eva didn't let that get too far. "Oliver!" she bellowed. He started and stopped only a few steps from the edge of a steep ditch.

"What the hell are you doing? Don't get ahead of us," Eva hissed.

The forest was extremely dense, now. The trees seemed to huddle together, edging closer and closer to one another with each step. They'd chased the horses away in their bid for concealment, but now Oliver wanted nothing more than to walk on something else's feet. He felt they were inching their way forward, each step taking them nearly nowhere.

"Wasn't supposed to be like this," he groused, not for the first time. Kendall and Eva had long learned to let him work through it on his own. He was the least able of any of them to cope with bare handfuls of mystery berries for their dinners and had never been an outdoorsman in the best of times.

They stopped one last time before the town, having learned to approach in the light of day. Still no fire allowed, they fell into easy routine.

The sudden sound of crackling snapped him out of uneasy sleep before his watch came up. He opened his eyes to oppressive darkness, the shape of Kendall's body barely visible curled nearby, and an upright moving shape that revealed itself to be Eva when she shook Kendall's shoulder and eased her to sitting with barely a sound. There was a creaking Oliver couldn't identify, growing louder as it approached. How many times now had they been followed or ambushed? It almost felt routine by now. He readied himself to bolt.

They huddled together on the forest floor, clutching at each other.

The wagon passed close by but seemed oblivious to their presence. Two lanterns hung from either front corner, and two men sat in the uncovered driver's seat. As scary as it was, it was an easy sign that they were drawing dangerously close to Nimblepine, especially if a wagon was bold enough to continue on so late into the night.

As they disappeared through the trees, Oliver let out a breath he hadn't realized he was holding. They settled back down, realizing then that they'd strayed far closer to the road then they'd meant.

In the morning, they resolved to travel parallel to the road. They'd meet people in the town, anyway, and it was far less suspicious to approach on the road than through wilderness. As the day dawned and plodded on, they saw more and more wagons passing back and forth until, around midday, they encountered a line of men across the road, stopping each wagon as it passed.

"Fucking checkpoint. You've got to be joking," Kendall muttered. One of the gun-weilding men warily approached each wagon, checking papers and questioning the drivers. Oliver's head began to ache.

Together, they made their way further from the road, hoping to go around the checkpoint without having to stop. As they did, a wagon approached with prisoners in the back, their chains clinking with each bump. One of the three prisoners spoke clearly but so fast as to be panicked, brown hair matted with filth falling into his face.

"Hey, could use a drink, you know. Thirsty." He tapped a manacled wrist against the side of the wagon. "I ain't teachin' shit without a bath, either!" The man driving the wagon didn't so much as turn around.

"You hear me?" The prisoner's voice rang out distinctly across the road.

"No manners on that one," the driver said lazily to the approaching guard. Another prisoner lunged to the end of his chains, mouth open in a snarl that revealed an empty mouth.
"Hey." A whisper came so close to Oliver's ear that he could hear the breath behind it. He whipped around, nearly cracking his head into Kendall's.

"You okay? Come on, Eva found us a way around.

They caught up to Eva, who greeted them with a disgusted expression. "Those were hardly guards. Did you see? Mostly likely farmers without proper training. Still, we should lie low."

They made their way up yet another hill which wrapped around one side of the town. At the top, the true scale of Nimblepine was revealed. Oliver had thought it would be a small settlement, maybe a village like New Haven all those miles back, but it instead sprawled out below them. Two huge warehouses sat on either end of the town, and from them rose the twin columns of smoke they'd seen from a distance. Close up, the columns were thick and dense, drifting slowly but continuously upward.

"What the hell could they be making?" Oliver whispered. Kendall shrugged, her eyes wide.

"According to our research, they have the capacity to weld and manufacture weapons, but the amount of exhaust is a little daunting," said Eva. "We should keep our eyes out when we get down there."

As they neared the outskirts of Nimblepine, the trees thinned and the first buildings came into clearer view. They slowed down then, walking along the edge of the buildings and hoping to find an alley to slip into.

A hand gripped the back of Oliver's neck with such force that it drove him to his knees. He tried to twist his head to the side, but was only able to turn enough to see the hand belonged to Eva before she shoved him with all her weight down to his belly in the underbrush. They'd wandered too close to an open plaza between the buildings, where a crowd of people was gathered around a raised platform. A large wagon filled with chained people stood behind the platform, and the bustle suggested the start of an event.

Nearby, at the edge of the crowd, a teenage boy and an older man in a red leather vest were talking beside a smaller wagon. And behind the crowd alone stood a large man in all black, just standing. Oliver saw the boy's face split into a smile of pure joy.

"Really?" His voice carried far and wide.

"Well, why do you think we rode all this way, my boy?" The man laughed heartily and clapped the boy on the back, and they drifted further into the crowd.

Eva's hand moved from the back of his neck to his arm, where it squeezed and hauled him in an awkward crawl along with she and Kendall as they inched away. He tried to steal glances back at the people, but the trees and plants blocked most of his view.

A whip cracked. "400!" a man yelled. "410!" They stopped abruptly as the crowd murmured and another few people passed close by.

"Look at her, sirs and madams," said a man from the auction platform. "Just look at her! One in a million, she is. What'll I get for her?"

They started moving again. Oliver saw flashes of the woman through the underbrush, her face still and even. He tried to stop, to resist Eva's pull to get a better look, but she clamped down so hard he felt his arm would break and forced his head around to meet her eyes.

"Get caught and I will leave you here." She hissed through gritted teeth, rage pooling in her eyes. His own anger nearly got the best of him, pent up resentment and exhaustion from the past weeks making his chest and throat burn.

"Quiet," Kendall grunted beside them, and Oliver let himself be dragged away.

They stayed a little farther from the outskirts after that, getting a little closer every once in a while to track their progress. As they neared the far end and the second warehouse loomed into view, a strange sound echoed toward them down a brick-paved road.

The unmistakable sound of an engine bounced between the houses, its originator zipping between gaps in the buildings, barreling toward them.

"Go!" Eva screamed, and they scattered, but not fast enough. The machine was on them: a compact wagon with a tube-shaped frame, three wire-spoked wheels, and a rumbling engine at its front. It moved faster than they'd seen anything in this time move so far. Faster, Oliver thought, than even the horses.

Oliver managed to scramble behind a tree to avoid being run over. The machine came to a screeching stop, then began to amble much more slowly back toward the road, its pilot hollering apologies into the open air. Oliver immediately recognized the large man in black from the auction, and he emerged from behind the tree in time to see another person in the back of the vehicle with a bag over their head, bobbing along as the car rolled over uneven brick.

"That–that wasn't a car, was it?" Eva's head appeared in his peripheral vision, echoing his thoughts exactly.

He felt the anger rising again, this time bolstered by the days and weeks of utter confusion. All the training they'd done meant nothing. This strange world had too many secrets their books and lectures left out. He saw that anger reflected in each of the womens' faces, which comforted him somewhat.

They walked on for another few yards when a howl broke through the trees, and a group of men appeared in their path. The crew turned to go around them but found more men trapping them in.

"Uh, hello!" Oliver called. One man stepped out from the line and approached them.

"You all are trespassing here."

"My apologies, sir. We'd be happy to get off your land if you'll just point us in the right direction."

"Not sure I want you off my land quite yet." He leered at each of them.

"I'm happy to offer all the money we have, if you'll just–" Eva started, but the man's foot shot out and connected with Oliver's diaphragm, knocking the wind from him and sending him to his knees. Kendall screamed.

"Well, we'll be taking that for a start." An arm came down around his neck, squeezing around his throat. He tried to claw at it, squirm, and bite at it, but the man it belonged to only laughed and squeezed ever harder.

Dogs began to pass back and forth behind the man who had approached them. He now looked at Eva. "Can you walk?" His chuckle was a dry, nasty thing, and he gestured back to his horse.

"Here ma'am, you can take my horse. Ride up to the gates, tell them I sent you. They'll let you right in." Laughter erupted around him, and Oliver saw him advance again as his vision began to fade. He felt himself being hauled upward, the grip around his neck still iron, and something hard impacted with the side of his head.

There was a bare moment of consciousness, some time later, in which he felt his hands and ankles tied painfully together. He tried to open his eyes, but instead fell once again into the void of unconsciousness.

Terry.
18??

He could hear the sea: a mighty roaring as the wave grew and grew, loomed over him, blotting out the sun. He whipped around, nearly falling prone in his haste, and found himself still in the forest, the roaring not the sea but the wind rustling the trees against each other. The sun not blocked by water but replaced by the moon and a million stars that glittered down at him wherever they peeked through the leaves.

Crickets droned. A bird called off in the distance. He turned back around and continued his pained slog through the rocks and brush. The tugging in his belly was insistent now, almost painful. More to the right. Climb over that stone. In and out. Duck the low branches. Use the trunk to pull yourself up. We gotta be fast. Slide down the other side. Bend your knees on impact. God doesn't make mistakes.

A woman's voice prodded at him as he climbed, perhaps from a dream. He couldn't recall her name or why she spoke to him. When he closed his eyes against the pain in his head, glimpses of her face flashed past him.

In and out. It took him several moments to realize that he was heading down the cold, clammy passage of a cave. It twisted and turned, narrowing at some points so he could rest a palm on either door and use them to propel himself forward. We gotta be fast. When the passage widened, he sometimes heard water dripping in the distance and feel the distant roar of an underground river. God doesn't make mistakes. He stumbled blindly forward, always forward, allowing himself to be compelled by whatever was drawing him in. His hand brushed a series of grooves, too regular to be natural. Running his fingers over the symbols, he felt some give in the stone and pushed it into the wall. There was a sliding and a click, then he felt some sort of stick or pole come jutting out, then another series of clicks, a spark, and the end of the stick burst into flame.

The flash of light shocked him for a moment, and he had to close his eyes against the wave of pain through his head, but then he took the torch, grateful for its warmth and a refuge from the darkness, and continued on. As he turned the last corner, he saw it. He felt it warm as he approached. Neither metal nor stone, but smooth and gray, he disappeared into the rock around the passage.

Eva.
18??

They rode through the night; hooves splashed puddle water dangerously close to her face. Before the men had roughly tied a blindfold over her eyes, Eva had noticed that they didn't seem to be in any kind of rush and recalled the group travelled in a kind of loose formation. The forest remained dense and cool around them, and though the men were rough and coarse, they made sure the three had food and water when the rest of them did. At mealtimes, their heads were uncovered and their hands unbound so they could feed themselves, though they were closely guarded and not allowed to stand or walk away by themselves.

"No worries now, none of y'all gon go hungry." The man in charge, thin as a stick but hard as steel, helped them as gently as he seemed able to down from the horses to sit against a tree. His eyes were nearly black and his hair and beard were stringy. When he smiled at them, he revealed

a few yellowing teeth propped against one
another.

"One of us might," Oliver muttered, turning
the gray hunk of meat he was handed this way
and that.

"Aww, come on. Can't have you all getting
sickly on me," the man spoke almost gently, as if
to an obstinate child, and set a man to watch over
and ensure they finished their meal.

The man looked disdainfully down at Oliver.
"I hear you folk on the other side of the hill like
horse better than chicken. This shouldn't be any
trouble for you." Oliver looked up, horrified, and
the man broke into dry laughter. The leader,
though close by, only watched while impassively
chewing his way through his own meal.

As they continued on, there was some relief in
not having to walk themselves, but riding a horse
propped up at the back of a saddle was
considerably less comfortable than riding astride
it. Eva made it her sole mission through those
long stretches of riding to keep the other two
always in her sight, twisting and turning, enduring
barks of reproach and even the occasional open
hand across the back of her head to pass her gaze
continuously between Kendall and Oliver. As
long as she could see them, they were still
together, and as long as they were together, they
would be okay.

But even as she tried to reassure herself, she knew staying together wouldn't save them. Her head still ached from the blow someone had cracked across her temple when they were ambushed. She'd watched Oliver go down, then Kendall, then had seen nothing but black until rough hands were pulling her knife and ration pouches from her pockets. She tried to struggle, but got nothing but another blow to the head for her trouble.

Now, though, she sat with a hood over her head, and though she saw Oliver and Kendall at meal times, she would no longer be able to tell, as they rode, if the group were to suddenly split up. When it rained, she breathed with difficulty through the wet cloth, but still they didn't remove it.

"Moon Reys! Up ahead!" A man shouted near the front of the formation. Orders began pinging between the members of the unit, and Eva was abruptly lifted from the horse and dropped unceremoniously on the wet ground. She felt two bodies come down behind and beside her.

"Like we practiced!" A horse's hoof clipped her foot, and she yanked her knees up against her chest.

"Leo, guard the Gems!" The shape of a man came to stand over them, facing away.

"Hey!" Eva struggled to try and pull the hood off. "Arm us! Help!" No one answered, and the man only stepped out of reach of her flailing legs. Then a cry rose into the air, and there was the thundering of even more hooves, the sound of gunfire, and the yell of men trying to rally one-another.

Eva managed to clamp a corner of the hood between her knees and pull it part way off of her head. The first thing she saw was one of the men who had captured her lying in the dirt, the lower half of his left leg nearly gone. She couldn't tell if he was the one set to guard them, but everything around them had turned into a battlefield. Men rode out to meet the Moons, then circled back to reload and launch themselves out again. She adjusted her grip on the hood and was able to pull it all the way off, then turned to Kendall and Oliver beside her and hissed, "Lean your head over. Let me get the hood off." With her teeth and some squirming by all of them, she was able to remove their hoods, and then she nodded to the man's body and Oliver leaned out to pull the hilt of a knife out of his remaining booth.

Sawing through their restraints was long and agonizing. They had to stop any time a man came by their hiding place, but they all were too preoccupied with the fight to notice or care about their lack of hoods or the strange way they were bent over one-another to pick at the knots.

Eventually, finally, they got Eva's hands free and she went about untying the rest of the rope. From there, she hauled Kendall and Oliver to their feet and together they scrambled onto and through the pile of boulders at their back, hoping to run in the opposite direction using the battle as cover. They found another man, once perched high with a rifle pointed down toward the Moons, now squirming futilely on the ground, blood pouring from his mouth and the front of his shirt soaked in it. Eva lowered her eyes and made quick work of searching him for another knife, and then followed Oliver and Kendall down the other side.

They were greeted by two men on horses and one on foot, all three with weapons trained on them. The sound of gunfire had stopped.

"You hurt?" one asked as they were led to sit and tied again. None of them answered aloud, but all three shook their heads curtly.

"Now, we ain't mad at 'ya, but we just wanna make sure you don't go doin' that again," he said, tightening the ropes so that they made Eva's hands and feet tingle. "We'll be gettin' rid of this, too," he said, fishing one of the knives she'd found out of her boot and throwing it lazily away. Oliver had already been relieved of the other—he hadn't thought to hide it in time.

"Save all yer foolin' and yer tricks for later," said another, leaning back in his saddle.

"Let's go," said the last. Another horse was rounded up, and once again they were lifted onto the backs of the saddles uncomfortably away.

They passed a camp of men who seemed to be packing up to set out. They glanced up and waved vaguely as the part passed, but didn't seem to pay any more mind. Then they crested a last ridge, and Eva felt horror crash through her.

Emerald Ranch sprawled below them, but she didn't have time to take in the vista before they were cantering down and through the fields. They passed laborers both black and white working in the fields, leading oxen and horses. A woman played with a child in one of the irrigation ditches, and she heard the child laugh below her. Strangest of all, a group of women sat in a circle in a wide patch of grass, what appeared to be a teacher or storyteller standing in the center gesturing widely.

It wasn't the plantation she had expected to find, and she twisted to catch Oliver and Kendall's eyes. They met her blankly, flinching together when thunder rolled, then together turned back to gaze in awe at the people they passed.

Lewis
1861

"We hide from outside eyes, guided by the dawn and the moon," Kyro continued, his voice low and resonant. "Watch your step." Lewis was too busy staring back and forth between the men they traveled with, and his foot caught on a hidden rock.

Walking through the forest felt more like an extended interview than a welcome. He and Sam had barely been able to get in an extra word between answering questions and hearing Kyro explain their rules and customs. Lewis was getting tired of learning new rules.

"So, tell me Lewis, where did you two come from?" Kyro's voice was always light and conversational when he asked a question. Any threat or warning he meant was carried in the bodies of the men traveling with them. For every

one visible, Lewis knew there were two or three
more traveling above, out of sight.

"A plantation near the river."

"Why keep running?"

"Uh," Lewis shrugged and looked to
Sam for help. "Freedom." It felt stupid and
obvious, but Kyro nodded seriously and fell into
contemplative silence.

As they walked, Lewis eventually worked up
the courage to introduce himself to two of the
men walking close by. Arlyn and Rufio were eager
to share their stories, once Kyro gave an
approving nod. They told of hidden underground
rivers, places where the trees grew so thick and
tall that you'd go days without seeing the sun,
caravans of travelers struggling across wide open
deserts. Rufio's favorites were the stories of secret
meetings and messages passed from man to man
across hundreds of miles. Arlyn was more quiet,
but interjected with important tidbits at the right
moments. It wasn't just messages they carried, but
people. The people hadn't redirected the river, the
land itself rose up and turned the water to keep
them safe.

They and Kyro were the only two who stayed
constant the whole journey. Others faded away
into the dark, replaced by newcomers who
whispered in Kyro's ear, exchanged small pouches
of goods or money, greeted Sam and Lewis and
exchanged hushed conversation with Arlyn and

Rufio. Once, Lewis thought he saw a knife made of pure gold flash between someone's hand and Kyro's pocket, but he didn't ask questions, and neither did Sam.

"I have a question for you," Kyro said on the second morning of their journey. Lewis noticed they always took their time getting up and about, as if they were waiting for something, and then, once that something occurred where Lewis couldn't see, they all were packing up and trudging along again.

"About strength." Lewis barely caught Rufio rolling his eyes behind Kyro. "What exactly does it mean to you?" Kyro looked between Lewis and Sam.

Lewis was, for once, at a loss for words. Strength wasn't something he thought about past keeping his own up in hard times. He thought Sam was strong, and Kyro, and many of the men he'd met and worked alongside. But it was clear, this wasn't the kind of strength Kyro was asking about. Body strength didn't need any explanation.

"Getting what I want from who I want, when I want," Sam chimed in first, his voice steady. Kyro looked at Lewis, who just nodded and gestured to indicate what Sam had said.

Rufio came up behind Kyro and tapped him twice on the shoulder. Kyro turned his head slightly and nodded, then gestured for Lewis and

Sam to stand and follow him. "Strength, as I see it, is freedom, but you'll see when we get there." They walked for barely an hour that morning before the trees began to thin and the sunlight warmed Lewis' shoulders. A rough dirt path emerged from the brush, and they fell into line along it down the slope, and around a bend, and in the sky above he could see a thin line of smoke drifting up into the clear sky. And there, at its base, was a respectably large log cabin with two steps up to a porch that wrapped around two sides, and an open, inviting door.

"Cabin belongs to a couple'a friends of ours who helped us a few years back." Arlyn flashed a derisive look over his shoulder. "Ehh, a little run-in.

"Anyway, since then, this is one of the places we stop to rest and organize. They're good people. You'll like 'em."

As they drew closer to the cabin, and everyone else's steps got quicker, Lewis felt his stomach tighten. Suddenly, all of this seemed too fast. Neither he nor Sam knew where they were. He'd been comforted by the fact that every new man they'd met was black, but even then they were strangers. There was no telling what they were being led to. He felt Sam nearly step on the back of his foot and quickened to keep pace. Too late now.

The cabin itself was built from sturdy logs, its surfaced weathered and grayed by the years. The roof was a patchwork of new and old wooden shingles, some coated in lichen and moss, and some so bright they could've been put on that morning. Smoke rose steadily from a stone chimney, and a dim glow could be seen through the open front door even in the sunlight. As the first man's foot fell on the lower step, a face appeared through that doorway and split into a wide smile, calling greetings and inviting them all in.

Edd Olson was tall and lean, with short, graying hair that spoke to years of labor. His face was lined, but his blue eyes sparkled with a kindness that put Lewis somewhat at ease. He shook Lewis' hand vigorously and warmly ushered he and Sam to meet his wife.

Marie Olson was much like her husband: lean, blue-eyed, and eager to greet them. But she was shorter and carried in her apron pockets all manner of small tools and utensils. She turned from a counter, where she was mixing a bowl of something thick and sweet-smelling in a wooden bowl.

After introductions all around, they were ushered into sturdy, mismatched chairs, and hot cups of tea pressed into their hands. Lewis thanked them but remembered his suspicion. The Olsons seemed more than kind, and he would happily accept their comfort and rest, but he would keep his eyes open and his wits about him, ready to move on if the time came.

They ate and talked. Plenty of laughter and the appearance of a cake, which Marie produced to applause, soon found Lewis relaxing. That night, he lay in a real bed, staring at the ceiling of a room only he and Sam shared with their own fireplace, warm and full and comfortable.

It only took one full day at the cabin to squash the last flicker of doubt. By the second night, he lay thinking of the warm light of the fire, the stew Marie had made and served them, the vast acres of fields and gardens.

He woke up later that night, slipped his feet into warm slippers, and went to find a cup of water. He found Kyro, Arlyn, and Rufio in the kitchen silently gathering their belongings. They looked up when he entered, but didn't speak, just hefted their packs on and filed out the door. Lewis followed a few steps, and then called softly to Kyro.

"I've been thinking about what you asked—about strength." Kyro looked at him steadily. "I've realized it's more than just getting what you want." He paused and shuffled, the chill of the night breaking through his thin sleeping clothes. "It's about having the freedom to make choices. To live without fear."

Kyro clapped a gentle hand over Lewis' shoulder. "That's a good realization. Freedom is the truest form of strength."
"Your stories—everything—they've given me a new perspective."

"Good. Enjoy the comfort for a while, but staying here too long can make you complacent. Freedom isn't always comfortable." With a final nod and a shake of hands, Kyro turned to leave, following Arlyn and Rufio into the dark. Lewis went back inside, drank deeply, rinsed and replaced the cup, and nestled back into his bed.

He knew that pursuit of the freedom he and Kyro had discussed would be his guiding star. He would stay at the farm for a while, freely exchange room and board for help around the farm, and then set out to find his strength. For the rest of his life, freedom would be the only master he served.

Kenny
1872

The night sky was ablaze with an orange glow. Kenny and Max stumbled through the woods, their senses dulled by the shock of the explosion and their ears still ringing. They had fled the burning wreckage of the Rolling Dice, not knowing where the rest of their team might be. Feeling the world dip and spin around him, Kenny caught himself against a tree, gasping. Max stopped a few steps ahead and collapsed to the grass, his face a mask of disbelief and shock.

"Keep moving!" A voice called behind them, breaking through the ringing in Kenny's ears. Simmons. He emerged with Steve and Juelz, their faces pale beneath a shadow of soot. Juelz limped with an injury Kenny couldn't see. Simmons huffed and heaved. Only Steve retained some of his composure, his fine coat pulled tight around him and his hands hidden in pockets.

"We have to keep moving." Steve kept his voice low, but a thick stripe of agony ran under it. "That—" he turned to gaze wide-eyed at the inferno, "that'll surely bring more lawmen." He winced and shifted his weight, then hauled Max to his feet and led them on.

The group plunged deeper into the woods, the roar of the burning train fading behind them.

"Behind—" Kenny's voice cracked as he tried to call loud enough for everyone to hear. Steve's head whipped around ahead of him and he nodded. Behind them was the clamour of hooves and mens' voices casting back and forth, searching for them.

"We need to find a place to hide," Simmons panted. "We'll never outrun them like this."

They all nodded, grim-faced. "There should be a stream up ahead," said Steve. "Might lose 'em in the water." Max was silent, his eyes fixed on the ground in front of him. Jeulz plowed through the underbrush with no regard for his clothes or legs. Kenny was no stranger to running, but this was different. The forest was close around them, the dark deepening with every step.

"Head for the ridge!" Juelz voice came from the trees ahead of him. They all quickened their steps, the sound of the Pinkertons and their horses ever louder behind them.

At the top, still sheltered by the tree line, they huddled and shook hands all around.

"We need to split up." Steve said and was met with a chorus of grim nods. "Lose 'em. You shake loose, regroup at the cabin up north." Kenny saw his own anxiety reflected in the faces around him. They exchanged final well-wishes, nods, and split up in different directions.

Kenny plunged into the thickening forest. Looking back after a few steps, he had already lost sight of the others, and the weight of his solitude settled heavily on his shoulders. He moved swiftly, his steps careful but quick, and all his senses on high alert.

The sounds of the Pinkertons remained faint but persistent behind him, and the trees and brush around him were alive with animal and insect sounds. He found a deer trail and began to follow it, hoping to get out of their search area and rest.

A scream pierced the night. It was close, too close, and Kenny couldn't tell if it was human or animal. He froze, crouching below the height of the underbrush. The scream turned into a gurgle, then a rustling of leaves so close he could see it.

He crept a few steps closer and squinted through the gloom. There was a figure writhing on the ground wearing the uniform of a Pinkerton. He revelled in the small victory, hoping that one of the others had gotten him, but confused that another could be so close by.

But then, the man began to convulse even more violently, a stream of insect bodies swarming up his sides and arms, enveloping him until their bodies muffled and then drowned out his screams. Kenny watched, frozen in horror, as the shape of his body disappeared under a carpet of shiny carapaces and became indistinguishable from the rest of the forest floor.

He didn't have time to process what he saw, and he finally noticed the approaching footsteps behind him.

"Over here!"

"Create a perimeter! Find him!" one of them commanded, dangerously close.

Kenny turned to tiptoe away, careful to step silently. Ducking around a tree, he almost collided with Simmons, and had to clamp a hand over his own mouth not to scream. Simmons stopped in his tracks, face ghostly in the moonlight. They'd gone in different directions, how could they have found each other again?

"What is happening?" Simmon's whisper was barely audible.

Kenny gave an exaggerated shrug and mouthed back, "Keep moving."

Every shadow now seemed a threat, every noise a danger. Every time his foot caught on a root, or a leaf or step brushed his legs, he slapped frantically at himself, imagining a carpet of bugs climbing his body to consume him.

They saw another Pinkerton through the trees, creeping forward with his firearm drawn. Kenny hooked a hand over Simmons' shoulder and pulled him to a stop, pointing. Simmons tried to turn and flee back the way they'd come, but Kenny stood his ground.

The Pinkerton began swatting at the air then began to jerk and yelp, then he crumpled to the ground. The shine of his face was quickly snuffed out by a swarm of insects, and then the dark made it impossible to see any more. Simmons gagged and his eyes darted to the ground around his feet.

A chill went down Kenny's spine. He yanked Simmons forward, breaking into a run. The forest around him seemed to pulse with malevolent energy.

They passed another body, a body entirely still as bugs crawled in and out of his eyes, ears, and mouth. There was faint yelling behind them—cut-off screams and men yelling for order.

In their panic, they broke through a hedge of tall plants, and Kenny's next step met only air. He tumbled down, tasting dirt, and landed hard at the bottom of a trench. For a moment, he lay there, too exhausted and stunned to move.

He blinked and lifted a hand to rub across his head. When it came into his view, it was shiny and writhing with insect bodies. He shook it, dislodging them over his own face. Panic surged through him, and he tried to scream, but before the sound could come, his mouth was full of scurrying bugs. He clawed at his own face, whipping his head back and forth, desperate to rid himself of the bugs. They continued to pour down his throat. A sharp pain began in his right ear, then his left, and he found he couldn't breath even through his nose.

The pain was agony beyond what he knew he could comprehend. His eyes and sinuses buzzed with them, his hands and belly, then behind his eyes and inside his head. His body jerked involuntarily. The world around him started to fade as the insects continued. He felt as if he were burning slowly, his entire body being consumed all at once. His thoughts condensed to single words, then sifted away entirely like sand.

Eva.
18??

In the distance, an unidentifiable building towered over the ranch, held up by huge white columns. As they trotted closer, Eva hoped they would go inside and find everything as she remembered. The outside of the ranch wasn't as she knew the Mundus headquarters in this time to be, but she could still hope that it hadn't been taken over entirely. She let the hope linger, knowing that, if the headquarters still stood unmolested, they would have been riding in under their own power.

They passed flags hoisted proudly atop flag poles, none of which had ever been there before. A deep green border dotted with symbols Eva didn't recognize lined each flag.
"We can't go in there," Oliver yelped after they had made it a few yards past the sign. "We're not–we can't go in there!"

The man sitting in front of Oliver on the horse smirked but didn't slow down.

People pointed and stared as they crossed the yard. Two older women stood beneath the eaves of a small building and brazenly followed the horses a few steps down the path, gesturing at them.

The party pulled to a halt in front of a barn and one-by-one were taken off of the horses' backs and the cords around their ankles cut to allow them to stand and be led.

"You. Name?" A man in a suit stepped out of the barn and addressed Oliver..

He nearly hesitated too long. "Uh, Joey." The man looked Oliver up and down once, then gestured to the man who had brought Oliver in.

"Fields–Asher has an open slot on the lower section."

"Yes sir, Mr. Marlon," and Oliver was hauled away. Every other step, he tried to turn back and plead desperately with Mr. Marlon.

"Fields? I've never worked a field! I'll-I'll mess it up!" But Mr. Marlon moved on to Kendall and Eva without any additional ceremony.

"Who might you two be?" He looked between their faces. "You know what, doesn't matter." He shook his head dismissively. " Take one to the kitchens, uh, her," he gestured to Kendall, who was frozen in fear, huddled as close to Eva as she could get, "and uh, her to the stables.

It took no time at all for Eva to conclude she didn't care for such treatment. The stables, at least, held the possibility of swift escape, but the kitchens would likely be hard to get away from. She and Kendall exchanged a look and a small nod before they were separated. From then on, they'd do whatever was necessary to survive and find each other as soon as an opportunity presented itself. Once alone, it would be every man for himself.

"The kitchens are nice and clean," said a middle-aged woman who had materialized by Mr. Marlon. She gestured for Kendall to follow and produced a knife to cut the rope around her wrists.

"Yes, Ms. Sally, would you be so kind as to escort these fine ladies?" Sally nodded and cut the rope around Eva's wrists next, then looped an arm around one of Kendall's and gently led them away and toward a large, square farmhouse. Eva's anxiety hit another level. She knew the elevator to the underground base to be in the barn they'd just walked away from. The possibility of an intact Emerald Ranch Mundus base dwindled yet farther.

The house bustled inside, men and women going up and down the main stairs, in and out of each of the rooms, taking packages to and fro.

Two men leaned over the banister talking indistinctly, then noticed and called down to Sally just before they went through the kitchen door.

"When you're done with those Gems, we're to join up with Al and the boys. They're headed east toward Yorksmith–apparently lots to find over there."

"Al?" Sally sounded alarmed. "Al?"

"No, no. Little Al. He's got nice with Dorian, and we're goin' out to look for gold. Need you to look after Ma."

"Alright, alright," Sally waved her hand dismissively. "I'll get them settled and be right up."

Eva didn't recognize the name Yorksmith, but knew there was another, smaller Mundus base a few hundred miles east of Emerald Ranch. She hoped it remained intact.

"Ahhh, Sally! If I might take it from here." A man in a long white coat bounded lightly down the stairs behind them, and caught up to the three women just as Sally was leading them through the kitchen door.

"Well, I–"

"Not to worry, I assure you. These ladies have a special role, here." He gestured to Kendall and Eva and watched Sally's face expectantly. Sally looked at a loss, mouth opening and closing, looking between Kendall, Eva, and the man.

"O-alright. Uh, go on, then."

"Excellent! I'll talk to Mr. Marlon." That made Sally relax, and her smile returned. The man gestured for Eva and Kendall to step back into the main room.

"Dr. Kendall Strife," once Sally disappeared into the kitchen, the man raised a sheaf of paper with a list of names and tapped Kendall's. "I don't, uh, really know who you are, ma'am, but your expertise stood out to us."

Something seemed off about this man, and it took Eva a long moment of searching his face before she realized that she could see the blurred outlines of blood vessels through his skin. Even on his cheeks and the palms of his hands, where she shouldn't have been able to see anything, faint dark lines crisscrossed.

"I don't know what you think you're doing with your little game, here, but you need to let us go." Eva mustered as much anger as she could into her voice, but knew even as it left her that she hadn't been able to overshadow her own exhaustion. "When backup comes, they might be lenient." When she began speaking, the man turned his eyes to her face, listening intently as if she were saying something of the utmost importance. When she was done, he nodded thoughtfully and then raised the papers again. Eva thought she could see the lines in his face pulse rhythmically.

"I think you'll find here, at Emerald Ranch, that we're on the cutting edge of history-defying technology. And, with both of your help, I can only imagine how far we'll advance." He smiled widely, his tongue and gums only a few shades pinker than his blindingly white teeth, which looked razor-sharp. He went to a narrow table in the hallway and flipped around a picture frame, revealing a screen with data scrolling steadily down it. Eva felt her stomach drop. He gestured for them to follow him down the hallway, and Eva found her feet moving unconsciously. They passed into the hall, and suddenly the man was behind them, ushering them forward so they had no chance of escaping back into the main room.

"What's going on?" Eva felt nearly frantic. "Where are you taking us?" Again, the man listened rapt, his eyes trained dutifully on her face, then nodded and carried on as if she hadn't spoken at all.

"Here, we blend experiments between what we know and what we believe to be possible." They reached the end of the hallway, and the man circled around them to a bookshelf built into the far wall. "Progress is slow, it's true, but steady." He reached up and pulled a lamp mounted to the wall just beside the bookshelf. It slid an inch or so out of the wall and the bookshelf slid sideways into the wall, revealing a narrow staircase that spiraled downward. He released the lamp and it snapped right back into place.

Kendall hesitated and tried to step back, but again the man was behind them, and they were being silently herded down the staircase.

"You wouldn't believe how loud it is," the man sighed. "When I hunt–hunted. The sound split the night–otherworldly!

"And it only started when you all arrived." Eva frowned but resisted the bait. She could have sworn, down in the dimmer light of the staircase, that the veins and arteries under the man's skin had gotten clearer, pulsed more distinctly.

"My brother, Sylvester," his voice took on a wistful quality, "I tried to tell him about it, when it first began. The sound, it drew us in.

"So," he sighed, put-upon, "we made a pact. No more hunting, not since that day."

"The day we arrived?" Kendall's voice was small, and the man's mouth stretched into a grotesque, thin-lipped smile.

"Exactly. A fracture in the fabric of things–a shift. And then, well, they were all gone."

"Who," said Eva.

"The other hunters. They went crazy–tore each other apart. Sylvester and I barely escaped–had to put down a few ourselves, just to survive."

Eva let the silence linger for as long as she could bear, already feeling the weight of so many tons of earth above them. "All of them?"

He shrugged. "Not all, I suppose. I'm sure there are a few still out there–a lucky few like us."

"And then," the lights lining the staircase flickered faintly, "you appeared." Eva could feel his breath against the back of her neck as he spoke, but when she whipped around to shove him away, he wasn't there. He stared at her, amused, from a few stairs above.

"But I couldn't leave well enough alone, could I?

"I started searching for people like you, and here we are." He gestured to the dark walls. "We've accomplished marvelous things."

They reached a landing and were herded out into a large square room with doors and hallways branching off of every side. The lights were brighter here, harsher, making the man look as pale and translucent as he'd ever been. "Welcome to the heart of our operation. Welcome home."

"Where are you taking us?" Kendall's voice shook so hard it sounded like she might shake apart.

"Yes, that is the question, isn't it. Not to worry. We're almost there." Eva turned to face him, but his voice came from across the room instead, right next to a solid metal door. "Over here, please."

He pulled a remote from his pocked, pointed it at the door, and it swung open to reveal rows and rows of laboratory tables, shelves of glassware and full vials of ever substance imaginable. Lights blinked from a bank of monitors on the far wall. Some of the tables were occupied by more people in white coats who barely looked up when they arrived.

"Here we are at the DSMI, where steam powers more than just engines. Here, it powers dreams!" He swung his arms out in a flourish, then chuckled lowly to himself. "This department is dedicated to creating steam-powered machinery, transforming industries from textiles to transportation.

"Notice," he skipped over to a schematic hung on the wall, waving a finger like a wand, "the intricate design of the steam engine model here. It stands testament to the revolutionary work you are here to be a part of."

He scurried to a far door and held it open for them to pass into another hallway, practically vibrating with giddiness.

"Over here!" He pointed into a doorway a little ways down the hall. "Next stop: Energy! It's not just coal and steam anymore. Here, we're exploring sustainable options for a brighter future."

The more he talked, the more his excitement ballooned until he was speaking nearly too quickly to be understood, pointing into each room they passed and explaining their purposes.

"Over here, we venture into medicine and biology. Medical treatment, advanced understanding of the human body, you name it."

They reached the end of the hallway, where it took a right-angle turn and branched into more hallways.

"To conclude our tour, a special final stop. Here is where we balance our books, so to speak, and make sure each program receives the funding it needs to be successful.

"And I," he gave a low, exaggerated bow, "am Dr. Hodges. It is my honor to welcome you to your new home."

"No." Eva said, shaking her head emphatically. "No, this isn't right. We can't–" She grabbed Kendall's arm, turned, and ran back down the hallway. Without looking back, they pelted past all the doors Dr. Hodges had shown them, through the lab amidst a chorus of startled and angry noises, and burst out into the square room, then stopped short, colliding with each other as they both tried to stop and turn back through the door, but it slammed shut behind them.

"Now, now," said Dr. Hodges, standing a few feet from the bottom of the spiral staircase. He shook his head admonishingly, looking at them with mock pity. "You've just arrived."

Sam

1861

The farm, he discovered over the first few days of their stay, required precious little upkeep. Edd Olson, though getting on in years, tended his fields and animals with a strong and expert hand, and the gardens were finely kept by his wife Marie. The worst was probably carrying water, which the Olsons couldn't do easily, but they were frequently stopped between buckets to rest and talk with them over snacks and the occasional hot cup of coffee. In these moments, Sam learned that they were the most recent in a stream of refugees brought to the farm, and that a few still lived there from time to time. It was a good, safe place to hunker down and plan your next step–the hills kept lawmen away, and precious few got too close to Mount Ulrich if they could help it.

"On account'a disappearances here and there," Edd had said. Then, perhaps seeing the looks on Sam's and Lewis' faces, flapped a hand at the looming mountain. "We've never had any trouble."

"Feels strange, doesn't it," Lewis remarked one evening as they sat on the porch, the sky awash with oranges and purples, "having a place to rest."

"Yeah," Sam replied, gaze fixed on the horizon.
"Hard to believe it's real."

Sam had to agree. Every morning they got up when they chose, were fed breakfast, and then they went about whatever chores they chose. They mended fences, split firewood, sawed some new shingles for the roof, and the couple always met them with profuse thanks and as much food as they could eat. Otherwise, they were left alone to do whatever they wanted. Lewis took to wandering the fields and forest. Sam took to napping in the house or the barn, and sometimes they sat and talked together, no need to whisper or hide, about what they might do after they left. "Where are you headed after this?" Sam asked one night. He'd taken to smoking a pipe while Lewis fidgeted with whatever interesting trinket he'd found on his walks.

"Don't know. I'll figure it out, though. It's worked fine so far." He shrugged and pocketed the stone, cut through with a thin thread of pink.

Sam had to admit to himself, he didn't know either, and he was increasingly unsure he wanted to leave at all. He found he liked being left to his own devices. He liked the regular food, soft bed, the pipe, and the company of the kindly couple.

One morning, a week or so into their stay, Lewis and Sam were washing up for lunch, and the crunch of wagon wheels came down the dirt road toward the cabin. The Olsons came out of their house and greeted the wagon with the same enthusiasm they'd met Sam and Lewis with. A black man sat in the driver's seat, waving back and directing the horse to pull up close to the house.

"Lewis, Sam! Come meet Juelz!" Marie called, helping Juelz down while Edd started to unhitch the horse.

Juelz turned and started toward them, hand outstretched to shake, but it quickly fell to his side while his face contorted into confusion and rage.

"You! The fuck did you do to me?" He was walking more quickly now, the open hand transformed to an accusing finger.

"Whoa, whoa." Edd's hand fell on Juelz's shoulder, but he shrugged it off and kept moving.

"We've never met you before." Sam took a sure step forward, raising placating palms toward Juelz. "I'm sure this is a mis–"

"Take me back motherfucker!" Juelz threw himself at Sam, taking them both to the ground. Sam struggled to kick Juelz off of him, but Juelz had a firm hold on Sam's shirt with both hands and had thrown his full weight. "You ruined my life!"

It took a moment for Lewis and Edd to pull Juelz up and away, where he stood behind Edd shaking with rage, still levelling a finger between Sam and Lewis. "Take me back."

"What are you talking about!" Lewis was clearly shaken, helping Sam brush twigs from his hair and then stepping clearly out of reach. Sam's chest and belly had gone cold with fear. He didn't recognize Juelz and believed that Lewis didn't either, but if Juelz had been in the Emerald Ranch group, he could bring any manner of chaos down on their heads.

"Juelz, these nice men don't know you." Marie tried her best to soothe, but Juelz brushed her off.

"Take me back. Now." He took a step toward Sam. Edd moved between them, but Sam still saw Lewis take off out of the corner of his eye.

He shot an apologetic look at Edd and Marie. "I'll find him. We'll come back." Then he set off running after Lewis. He immediately heard raised voices between Juelz and Edd, and then a short scuffle as he reached the edge of a field and plunged into the trees, following flashes of Lewis' back and the sound of his footfalls.

"Hey!" Jeulz' voice sounded behind him, faint, but getting closer. "Hey! Take me with you!"

Unfortunately, Lewis had chosen a path that led diagonally up the slope of the mountain and Sam soon cursed the burning in his legs and the rocks that threatened to trip him. He called after Lewis, trying to get him to slow, but Lewis only glanced back and continued on, pelting up the mountainside.

"Wait!" Juelz still hollered and crashed through the trees behind them. He was plainly faster than Sam and likely knew the terrain better, but the way Lewis zigzagged back and forth and Sam did his best to stay out of sight kept him at bay.

Sam checked behind himself for Juelz, saw nothing, and turned back around just in time to hear Lewis yelp and see him disappear behind a cluster of tall bushes.

"Lewis!" He instantly regretted calling out, hearing Jeulz call out again down below. He climbed to the place Lewis had disappeared as quickly as his burning legs could carry him, then cast around for a moment, thinking Lewis had tripped and slid down the slope in another direction. It took long enough for Juelz to appear. Too close for comfort, he stopped for a bare moment to scan for Sam, then began a beeline toward him.

"Sam." He heard Lewis' voice somewhere behind him, not fallen back down as he expected. He scanned the bushes, even brushing a hand through them, then saw Lewis lean out of a gap and gesture for him. "Come on!"

Sam clambered through the bushes and emerged in the mouth of a low, dimly-lit tunnel. He felt water rumble somewhere far into the mountain, and saw the walls, floor, and ceiling quickly disappear into flat darkness. He and Lewis exchanged an apprehensive look and then crept as carefully and quietly as they could into the darkness. After a few yards, they went around a bend and Sam put out a hand to stop Lewis and listen.

There was silence for a long moment, save for the distant sound of the water, and then a furious rustling and the crunch of shoes on gravel.

"Hello? You can't leave me here!" Juelz' voice ricocheted against the rock, seeming to come from behind them, in front of them, from the dark of the ceiling. Sam pushed Lewis into motion, and they took off into the darkness, stumbling and tripping, stubbing their toes and trailing one hand each against the wall.

Eventually, a warm light appeared around a bend. "Sunlight!" Lewis said lowly, and they slowed to approach.

As it came nearer, it became clear that they weren't lucky enough for an exit, but a nearly-extinguished torch, its cloth head rendered entirely to ash and its handle nearly gone. Sam removed his shirt and did his best to wrap it around what was left. Lewis helped him blow the dying flame onto the cloth, and then Sam hoisted the torch high to look around.

In the dim light, a shape lay sprawled in the opposite edge of the path, irregular and cloth-covered but smaller than either of them.

"Is that a body?" Lewis said, his voice echoing. They stepped a little closer, trying to get a better look, and the light fell over a furred hand with dark nails like claws. Lewis gasped and jumped back, colliding with Sam and forcing them both against the far wall. Pebbles rained down over them, then larger rocks, and then scrambled out of the way, crawling through gravel before getting their feet. By then, the rain of rocks had stopped, and they both stepped back toward the body, intent on further investigation.

Sam only made it two steps before the floor disappeared beneath him, he lost his grip on the torch, and they both went tumbling down into fresh darkness.

Kendall.
1861

More than two months in, if her estimation was correct, Kendall had already forgotten what it was like to wake up to the sun. Guards entered her small cell, their faces shadowed and unreadable, and unfastened her from the wall. She stood stiffly, put her feet into the slippers they had issued to her, and followed them and the small group of scientists they'd already retrieved down the hall.

The cells seemed to be in one of the upper floors of the underground compound, and as they descended, the quality of the light changed from dim to stark, humming white. The elevator creaked and groaned. Vincent, a quiet chemist from a few cells down, trembled and fixed his eyes on the ceiling.

Then the doors ground open and they stepped into the Theatre of the Mind, a huge labyrinth in the depths of the compound, its walls too high to see or climb over, and glass-sided observation decks dotted above it. Every day, three of them were chosen to participate in the trials while the others waited and watched. If they passed, they weren't made to participate the next day. If they didn't they ran the trials day after day until their overseers decided they'd made enough contributions to their research. So far, Kendall hadn't had to run the trials for more than a day in a row, but she dreaded the day she didn't complete them in time.

The trials, on their face, were simple: navigate the labyrinth. Unlock shortcuts by solving puzzles and putting together the materials they were provided in new and innovative ways. Hope for inspiration. Find the exit and succeed, or get lost in the labyrinth and wait for the guards to pull you out. Get out fast enough and earn extra recreation time while the others kept toiling. With each new success, the trial grounds expanded and the puzzles that faced them grew more complex and demanding.

"Welcome back," came the unenthusiastic voice of an overseer. "You all know how this works. Time and creativity are of the essence. Get stuck, go again tomorrow.

"You, you, and uh, you. Let's go." The guards unshackled Kendall, Paul, and an aquatic biologist named Alisa and led them to the starting platforms.

"And, go." Kendall stepped into the labyrinth, knowing by now that conserving her energy would get her farther than sprinting out of the gate. The air was stagnant and thick with the smell of something metallic. All around, the constant hum of machinery droned on.

"Stay close," she said to the other two. Paul was the newest of them, and this was his third day in a row on the trials.

They moved methodically through the turns and dead ends, eventually coming upon a large metal door with a panel of dials and levers to its left. Paul tried to twist the handle, but it didn't budge.

"Here," Alisa leaned down toward the bottom left corner of the door, where a mechanism drove a metal rod into the floor, preventing the door from opening.

"Mm, alright, get to work." They each took a section of the panel and began to work through all the possible combinations.
"Try 42, there, up, up, down." A loud buzz sounded above them.

"33 there, then 17, then 4. Switch that lever." Another buzz.

"33-4-12. Switch those two. No, the other one. Then switch that one back."
There was a ding and a sliding thud. This time, when Paul turned the door handle, it slid open easily.

They hurried through the door, the heavy footsteps of a guard echoing behind them. They traversed the maze a while longer, then came upon another door with a typewriter-like device with pipes coming out of every angle and disappearing into the walls and ceiling. Its keys shone a soft copper in the dim light. A small stack of papers sat beside the typewriter covered in letters with no discernable sequence. Valves and grates dotted the walls, some already trickling steam into the chamber.

They set to work checking each valve. Something clicked into place in Kendall's head. "We're trying to power the typewriter. Here. Divert pressure back that way." They worked fast, but still the room grew hotter and more humid, the system of pipes refusing the cooperate. Sweat dripped down Kendall's face, and she saw the guard come around a corner. Their time was running out.

Paul turned a valve wheel and the typewriter sprang to life, printing a portion of a cypher. He scrambled to begin decoding the message while Kendall and Alisa kept manipulating the pressure flow.

"Too high over here!" yelled Alisa. "Something's wrong!"

Kendall's heart jumped as she saw the gauge nearest Alisa spike dangerously fast. They were moments away from a catastrophic failure. The next wheel she touched was too hot to touch, so she went to the next one, shouldering Paul out of the way.

"Watch–" but it was too late. A jet of scalding steam shot out of a seam between two sections of pipe, hitting Paul right in the face. He screamed and crumpled to the floor. Kendall kicked at the burning wheel, inching it open bit by bit until the pressure dropped back to normal and the steam leak stopped.

The typewriter clattered behind her, printing the final piece of the cipher.

"We did it," she rushed over to Paul's side. "Are you okay?"
Paul was writhing on the ground, both hands clutched over his left eye. One hand was red and blistered, as was most of his face. The guard advanced, pressing into Kendall's personal space until she backed away, then wordlessly hauled Paul's uninjured arm over his shoulder and began to half-carry him back through the maze.

They knew the rules. Even if they succeeded, Paul would forfeit, and as soon as the medics deemed him fit to participate again, he would be back in the labyrinth. Kendall watched him until the guard rounded a corner and they passed out of sight, then went to meet Alisa where she had already decoded the rest of the message and unlocked the door.

More on edge than ever, they continued until they found yet another door, this one painted gold. These puzzles meant immediate release into recreational time for the rest of the day, but the test would be much harder than all the others. Kendall hesitated, but Alisa charged ahead into the room.

Inside the room was a single large workbench and a digital timer dominating one wall. It read, "01:00:00" in bright red numbers.

Dr. Hodges' voice came crackling through hidden speakers, "Welcome to the Prize Room. To earn your free time, you must create a functional electrical devise using the tools and materials provided to you." Kendall looked around at the shelves and boxes of scrap.

"We need to think of something simple but effective," said Alisa.

Kendall began rummaging through a box of rejected produce. "Can you find a small lightbulb?"

Alisa sprang into action. "You already have an idea?"

"Potato-powered light bulb."

"What? I don't think–"

"It'll be fast, at least," Kendall said, selecting a mostly-firm potato and moving on to piles of copper wire. "Just trust me. If it doesn't work, we'll have plenty of time to figure something else out."

Alisa set a bulb on the table. Kendall cut two lengths of wire and went about connecting them to the bulb while Alisa overturned boxes for galvanized nails. They worked in quiet sync, pressing the nails into the potato, wrapping the free ends of the wire around them, disconnecting and reconnecting the bulb when nothing happened.

Then, the bulb flicked to life, and they held their contraption aloft for the observation decks to see. The timer froze at "00:24:45".

"Congratulations, you're free for the day."

The far door clicked, and a guard appeared to escort them away. Kendall eagerly allowed the chains to be returned to her wrists, then followed the guard to the elevator and up into blessed sunlight.

The fresh air was a rare treasure that she vowed never to take for granted again. She and Alisa parted ways as they exited the elevator, each flanked by a guard, and Kendall wandered to a nearby oak and sat in its shade. She closed her eyes for a moment, feeling the breeze, and when she opened them a woman came walking across the grass toward her. The intensity of her eyes was unmistakable, and Kendall waved as she got closer.

"Afternoon, Hattie." She stopped a few feet away, her posture rigid.

"They told you yet?" She glanced mistrustfully at the guard.

"I told him to get out of the way. I just wasn't fast enough."

Hattie sighed and looked away. "Yeah, say what you want. Nobody deserves that."

Kendall did her best to make the most of the day. She lounged in the shade, watching the strange behavior of the yard's insects. Different species clumped together, seeming to move with the same purpose. She watched ladybugs follow ants to and from their colony, honeybees resting on the tree's bark beside a moth. She took out a pencil and the notebook she'd been given and began to record her observations.

Sometime later, after a trip to the house for food and water, she returned to the tree and looked out over the plantation. There, in the distance, she could see Eva training a class of new recruits. They hadn't been allowed to speak since coming to Emerald Ranch, but Kendall sometimes saw her from afar on days such as these. She wore a deep olive green shirt and fitted brown trousers, and indistinct snippets of her voice drifted to Kendall on the breeze.

Kendall admired Eva's dedication, but sympathized with the turmoil that must be happening below the surface. She felt she would never get used to life on the Ranch.

"Let's go," said the guard after a while more. She handed her notebook to him, and he flipped through what she had written. They were to have at least a page written each day, and she'd easily filled two. He nodded, handed it back, and they made their long way down into the belly of the plantation to Kendall's room. She stepped inside and let herself slump down onto the bed as the door slammed shut behind her.

Steve
1872

Screams cropped up around them, anguish hidden by the trees. Steve and Juelz kept up a near-run through the trees, Juelz babbling something about bugs and collapsing Pinkertons. Steve couldn't make any sense of it, but he didn't stop to try. He had no clue where they were or where they were going and was far more concerned with getting them safely away to the cabin.

They trotted along for hours, eventually not bothering to step quietly, until the screams fell far behind them and then faded altogether, but the world was not silent. All around them the ground, trees, and water they passed trembled, and a hum rose behind them. Leaves fluttered to the ground, shaken from the trees. Juelz tried to slow to a walk, but Steve took hold of his arm and pulled him none-too-gently along.

"This fuckin' day." Juelz muttered. "Where are we going?"

"Don't know." Steve could feel the hum in his chest and head. He imagined the ground shaking apart behind them and falling down, down, down to the center of the earth.

"Here!" It was Jeulz' turn to grab his arm and yank Steve toward a stony rise on their right, knocking Steve out of his panicked daydream.

"What—" Juelz ducked around a thicket of trembling leaves and disappeared. As he got closer, Steve finally saw the deep shadow of a little cave made by an overhang of dirt and roots. He stopped short of ducking in, watching the plants around its entrance shudder.

Juelz' head and shoulders reappeared. "We'll be safe here for now. Come on, plenty of room." The hum was so loud that Steve could barely understand even as Juelz yelled. He shook his head.

"Can't stay here." He gestured for Juelz to come out and follow him off in the direction they had been going.

Juelz came out, close enough for Steve to hear the panic in his voice. "Get it together, man. We're dead if we panic." He turned, motioning for Steve to follow.

Steve shook his head again, his eyes scanning back the way they'd come. Were those shadows always that dark?

"Something's coming!" He tried to get his voice above that deafening droning noise, but Juelz was already backing toward the cave again, the noise beginning to eat away at the last of Steve's resolve.

He turned and ran, crashing through underbrush and low branches alike, down into a valley and back up the other side, puffing like a freight train. He tripped and fell more than once, covering himself and his coat in mud, shredding it through thorn bushes, and always the sound of a million-milllion droning wings behind him.

Eventually, cresting the next hill, he was able to get enough of a bearing to correct his course. No longer so concerned with being followed by Pinkertons and desperate for the sealed windows and locking door of the cabin, he kept on due north.

He stumbled upon the stream and the little waterfall without hearing it. The hum still covered every other sound, even his own crashing footsteps. He allowed himself a small moment of relief to dip his hands in the water and splash it over his face, and then he was off again. Northeast from there. Soon, a small farm and a gap in the fence. Then, less than a mile straight out into the wilderness, the cabin. It took some doing to get the door open, and then he was inside, and he pushed the door firmly closed behind him.

The air was thick and smelled of old wood and mildew, but the outside hum was muffled enough to hear his own thoughts. He collapsed against the door and dropped his head in his hands.

He'd left Juelz out there all alone. Guilt rose like bile in the back of his throat. Not to mention the others. He shuddered to think what might have happened to them. He would have to go back–if he could even find his way–once the humming stopped.

He saw a small movement out of the corner of his eye, and looked down to see a single-file procession of dark-shelled beetles crawling under the door, just visible in the moonlight. Then another appeared next to it, and three more on his other side. He shot to his feet, stomping wildly, and took his coat off to shove in the crack under the door. Then he took out his lighter and began to clear the house, checking the seals around the windows and gathering any scraps of fabric he found to replace his coat beneath the front door. As he moved, the hum continued to rise, and then to fall as whatever was making it passed over the cabin and beyond. He shoved what little furniture could be found against the door, spread an old moth-eaten blanket out in one corner, and sat down to wait, closing his eyes and listening to the hum gradually recede.

He opened his eyes some time later to absolute silence. The sky was pinkish and beginning to lighten. His joints and back protested as he stood and went to the front window.

The first thought that came to him was that he'd gone mad. He rubbed a hand over his eyes and looked again, frozen in disbelief.

The trees seemed to bleed a tarry, black substance that had already pooled beneath them and was nearly halfway up the only step to the cabin's front door. Their trunks were coated with it, their leaves and branches sagging painfully toward the ground. The cabin was on the side of a hill, which should have meant that the inky liquid would flow away from it, but instead he watched it flow backwards over the top of the step and toward the base of the door, out of view of the window.

Steve gathered the blanket he'd slept on and shouldered the furniture aside to add it to the cloth under the door. Then he flipped the table he'd found on its side and slid the flat top flush against the door. It was a heavy table, probably left behind because it couldn't be easily loaded into a wagon, and he thought it might help seal the door.

But in just a few moments, the black ooze was seeping around the top of the table toward him, running through a crack he hadn't seen in the wall under the window, creeping toward him from other cracks behind and to either side. It didn't spread or flow like any other liquid he knew, but instead ran right toward him, as if drawn.

It felt then like the humming was coming from inside him, and with it the whisper of indistinct voices. He picked one foot up to avoid the first patch of it, and was forced to put it back down in the growing puddle. Immediately, it seeped into his shoes, cold and wet, and the whispers grew louder and nearer.

Eva.
1861

Drenched in sweat, Eva advanced toward Moe again. He was doing a poor job of defending his left side, and Eva hooked a sharp blow around the back of his left thigh, which jolted and went out from under him. He crumpled to one knee and looked up at her with a huff and a grimace.

"You all are the worst class I've ever trained." She made sure those in the back could hear her. "Men and women. All of you!" She lowered her voice and swiped a wrist across her forehead. "Unbelievable."

She was still surveying their sparring matches when a man ran up to her. "Ms. Eva," he gasped, nearly colliding with an out-of-bounds match. "We just got word: five more Gems by the end of the week–maybe even the next few days."

She tried her best to keep her face impassive, but didn't miss the way the Scarab smiled apologetically and cut his eyes away. "Thank you." He took off again and was replaced by James, a guard and her constant shadow.

"That's enough for today. Get rid of 'em—back at first light." She nodded and went about rounding everyone up and dismissing them. Then, she let James lead the way toward the large hay barn near the back of the property. On their way, as they always did, they stopped by the infirmary, and Eva was given enough freedom to duck her head in by herself.

The only one still around was Madilyn, their resident doctor, and Eva caught her attention and gestured back toward the training field.   "Some cuts and bruises training today."

"Be there in a moment. Take a candy." Eva reached into the bowl of paper-wrapped sweets, pocketed an oddly-shaped one, and popped another in her mouth. She emerged again, was immediately flanked by James, and off they went.

Near the back of the barn, James pressed the lower end of an inconspicuous wall panel, and there was a click and a soft clanking far below them. A mechanism in the floor began to rise, pushing the hay bales on top of it toward the ceiling. An elevator slowly revealed itself, mesh-walled and only big enough for she and James to stand shoulder-to-shoulder. They stepped in and waited the few agonizing moments for the elevator to lower itself again.

As they made their way slowly downward, the sounds of the ranch above faded out and were replaced by the clanking and whirring of the elevator and the high drone of the electricity that ran through every inch of the underground complex. She'd never seen the lights turn off, even deep into the night when they ran evacuation drills or most of the hundreds of staff were above ground. When a bulb burned out, it was replaced within minutes, and the sound of their filaments and the wires that connected them continued on.

She'd gotten used to the security department, recognizing the twin advantages and disadvantages of being placed there. She was housed in the innermost section of the compound, guarded closely, and was rarely alone, which made escape nigh-impossible, but at the same time she had see more of both the underground and aboveground compounds than most, and she had easy access to new recruits and got to hear their stories of the goings-on of the world around them. Not everybody got that, and she still cringed sometimes to think about the workers stuck down here for days at a time, sickly with lack of sunlight.

The elevator stopped and they got out at their floor's security checkpoint. The guards there patted her down, asked their regular questions—are you returning from a trip off-ranch; have you discussed Emerald Ranch, its location, or its employees with anyone not employed by the ranch; are you bringing anything with you that might be unauthorized—and she was passed into the care of two new guards. James gave a curt nod, re-entered the elevator, and disappeared toward the surface.

"Safety and security are paramount here at the Hodges Foundation," the guard at the desk intoned. By now, she'd heard that phrase and been through this very process easily a hundred times—even with these same guards—but still they persisted.

"And I endeavor to uphold it." She plastered a mocking smile across her face and fell into step between the two guards. They passed through a set of massive steel doors, nodded at the Scarabs stationed there, and set about through the labyrinthine hallways to Eva's room, where she was allowed to enter alone, and then the door was shut and she heard the lock engage from the outside.

That night, she lay awake, running through the map of the compound she'd constructed in her head. Tonight would be the night, after months of waiting and watching.

Shift change was promptly ten pm. She'd have roughly five minutes to get out and hide.

She unwrapped the oddly-shaped candy and emptied a few curls of discarded metal into the pile she'd already accumulated over her many post-training visits to the infirmary. Over time, she'd been working on picking the door's lock with the bits of metal, hammering and twisting the longer pieces into a pin and hook. There was no counting how many she'd snapped or bent past saving or nearly lost in the lock.

She pressed her ear to the door, listening for the retreating footsteps, then reached down to worm her improvised pick into the lock. It took some doing–careful feeling for the pins, counting and re-counting the number of pins, counting the seconds under her breath. And then came the give and click, and she eased the door open, heart pounding so loud she swore she could hear it.

Nothing. The hairs on the back of her neck prickled. She needed to get out of the hallway as soon as possible.

Down the hall, keeping low and light-footed, she checked around corners and avoided main corridors. One day, she'd needed an extra piece of equipment to train the Gems and the guards had led her to dusty, quiet corner of the compound near another entrance, where the doors led out into another series of natural escape tunnels rather than an elevator. She headed that way then, passing empty rooms where strange devices whirred and blinked. From there, she had to move more slowly, creeping from room to room, crouching behind empty desks to avoid the guards going to and from their patrols.

She was in a utility room two doors away, could see the heavy doors at the end of the corridor, could smell the earth outside, when alarms began to sound. She took a deep breath, then another, and steeled herself, digging her fingernails behind the cover of a large pipe. For a long, agonizing moment, she was completely exposed. Anyone who bumped the door open slightly would be able to see her, and the barking of dogs was beginning in the distance.

Finally, painfully, she wedged the cover off, and without stopping to look, wedged herself into the pipe and brought the cover back up behind her.

The metal was burning cold and bit into the exposed skin of her palms and wrists as she pressed herself as far back into the narrowing pipe as she could. The air was thick with a nauseating ammonia stench that made her eyes water and bile threaten the back of her throat. Footsteps rang across the floor, voices shouted orders, dogs barked and their nails scrabbled against metal. She didn't hear anyone enter the room, but realized too late that she couldn't see anything from her hiding spot and would have to open the cover, revealing herself, to check.

"North compromised. South's covered. Take east!" A commanding man's voice stopped in the corridor. She heard a low reply. "Best condition.

No harm comes to the Gems." Then boots were pounding away again.

The commotion continued for another few seconds, and the only sound was the alarm. Eva cracked the cover, peering out into the office, and saw no one. The door was still pulled-to as she'd left it. No shapes passed. Slowly, ready to shove herself back inside, she emerged and straightened, taking a deep, desperate breath. She went to the door and prepared to make her break.

They weren't looking for her. Whatever chaos was occurring at the entrances to the ranch, it's timing was more than impeccable. Even better, it had drawn all of the guards away. She took a moment to look up and down the corridor and then burst into motion, sprinting with all her might toward the door, around the desk to press the unlocking lever, and through the door and into the cool, merciful dark of the tunnels. She might actually make it.

The only way to go was forward, so that's where she went, trailing a hand along one wall to keep her bearings. There were no lights strung here except for one right outside the door, and its light quickly faded. She trailed one hand along a wall to keep her bearings and revelled in the cool, clear air.

The path diverged three times, and each time Eva took a path that angled upward. Soon, she could hear the sound of wind in the trees and even see faint moonlight above her. She emerged into a small clearing surrounded by trees, the tunnel emerging out of the sheer side of a hill.

She stepped out and sat heavily against a tree, relief driving the adrenaline out of her body. She felt as if she could sleep for days.

"Eva?" a silhouette materialized across the clearing, the glint of a shotgun barrel across its belly. Eva froze, new adrenaline crashing through her. Then the silhouette came closer, stumbling across the grass until Eva could make out the face and wild hair of Kendall. Her expression was anguished and her voice thick with tears. "Eva!"

Eva rose to meet her, and they clasped arms and stood there for a moment, taking in that the other was still alive, and then Kendall stepped back and gestured for Eva to follow. "This way." Kendall led the way down a narrow path, continuing their progress away from the ranch.

Eva knew that Emerald Ranch was at the base of Mount Ulrich and had no choice but to hope she could find the right stream to follow up into the mountain. For all she knew, she could be miles away from her goal, but she'd finally escaped and could do what had to be done.

As they walked, a teeth-grinding sound rose from the ranch behind them. A mechanical whirring and clicking, a shuddering, rhythmic pulse that made the mountainside feel alive and breathing.

They sped to a run, Eva taking lead up and up and up. They stumbled through a narrow stream and Eva spun in triumph to see Kendall was nowhere to be seen. She looked back and forth, scanning every inch of the forest for Kendal or the shine of her gun. The light of the ranch shone far and wide below her, tiny shapes dashing back and forth across its grounds.

"Eva!" She turned back again and just caught a glimpse of Kendall's anguished face, perched in the lowest branches of a tree, before a blunt pain exploded at the back of her head.
Every sound narrowed to a distant hum. Her visioned blackened, then a few points of light floated among the dark. She felt icy water splash up her arms and then over her face before closing over her head.

The points of light became strange landscapes on strange worlds. Cities built in smooth, arching architecture. Forests of mountain-tall trees. Then faces made of mist and clouds, mouthed words to her she couldn't quite make out. One drifted close, so close it filled her field of vision and then the mist washed over her and her lungs began to burn, her mouth full of icy water.
Her limbs flailed weakly. Too stunned even to panic.

THE ARCHITEKT

THE BRIDGE

Time and space twisted around them, a kaleidoscope of stars and darkness. For a moment, Terry forgot he was falling at all as lights raced to keep pace.

A floor, rushing up to painfully meet his shoulder and hip, reminded him, and in the time it took to squeeze his eyes shut in pain and open them again, the swirling light and chaos was gone. He'd forgotten what stepping across a Bridge felt like: horrible, but not unexpected for a doorway and a single step across the cosmos.

He stood up and was met with another unique aspect of the Bridge in the dilation it caused in the space around it. Looking back, no matter how far he got from it, it seemed only a step or two behind him, the stone of the wall behind it fish-eyeing around so when you looked at it it seemed like the only open path.

Around the door, a rough semicircle of canvas dropcloth was hung from the ceiling, shielding anyone on the other side from the disorientation it caused. Terry put a hand to the edge of a cloth to pull it back and felt a twinge of anxiety squirm in his belly. He hoped he wasn't coming back to failure.

"Everything is going to plan." He pushed aside the cloth and stepped into a small room lined in monitors and a few other doors. Sulisea stood bent over one module and didn't turn when he spoke. "Mostly to plan. It got away from me at–at the end." He stood awkwardly in the center of the room, waiting for her to acknowledge him.

There was a long, still moment, and then she spoke. "It's on–right here–it's working." She lifted one shoulder out of the way and pointed at a blinking green symbol on the monitor. "Just barely. The vessel appears to have been compromised"

Terry heaved a sigh of relief and stepped closer to her, peering where she indicated. Sure enough, the blink was slow and faint, but it was there.
Sulisea abruptly straightened. "Almost done there, then we can move on." Her voice had an undercurrent of urgency, but her face and stance were as sure and steady as a leader's should be.

Terry looked around. He'd expected there to be more celebration if they were succeeding, but none of the other members of their rescue squad were anywhere to be seen.

"They're waiting for us at the next Bridge. We were supposed to be in and out." She gave him a sharpish look. "Clean." Terry grimaced in apology. "Anything I should know before I go?"

"We Located the northwestern hemisphere Vessel as planned, made contact, got her in place. Didn't have as much time as we thought I'd have. There was an unexpected crash, and I got separated. Seems like she survived.

"I didn't get to lead her into town, but she's trapped there now." He squirmed under Sulisea's impassive gaze.

"The Vessel is on it's first lifetime sentence–probably reincarnating as we speak– with at least four more to go. She should still have spread the virus to plenty of people and redirect them by then." He stopped, and they both turned to a digital clock hung on one wall above the computers. It moved rapidly in months and years instead of minutes and seconds, and as they watched, centuries passed in a manner of minutes.

"There you go." Terry gestured to the clock. "Lifetimes all done. A couple million more vessels corrupted." He looked down. The green symbol was blinking more strongly, and a number had begun to populate next to it. It changed even more rapidly than the clock, and soon millions of people were infected with the nymph virus and ready for extraction.

Sulisea nodded and gave the smallest smile of approval, then turned and began systematically entering a sequence of code into each computer, and soon each module was set to proceed with the destruction of the vessels and extraction of each prisoner. They locked down each module, took one last look at the results of their hard work, and turned to leave.

Sulisea opened a door opposite the Bridge, and she and Terry jogged down a hallway, taking twists and turns Terry could have navigated in his sleep, until they arrived at a large, open room, this one also having a stone wall and a semicircle of canvas covering a doorway. As they burst into the room, a single cheering voice raised, and Terry saw Luna waiting for them by the curtain.

"The others?" Sulisea slowed and clasped Luna's hand.

"Safely through. I wanted to wait for you." Terry shook her hand as well, and then Luna held the curtain aside for Sulisea and Terry to go through first.

Though the Bridge was actually several meters from the doorway itself, Terry barely took a single step before he was being engulfed by the stars and colors of the Bridge. But instead of racing the lights to his destination, they grew and bled into each other until he was surrounded by a blinding expanse of white.

"No!" He tried to call into the void, but his voice was strangely flat and muffled. He whipped his head around, looking desperately in every direction, and realized he was standing on a firm, cool surface but saw nothing.

Then the light dimmed as a shadow loomed over him, and he cowered with his hands over his head, still unable to see anything but endless white. He felt the weight of eyes on his shoulders and head, and they burned with the intensity of that gaze. He felt he would go blind if he looked up.

You. Steal. From. Us? The words carved through the air, a cacophony of overlapping voices, each vibrating in an ancient, cosmic tone. Strings of silk, plucked to hear the answering hum.

He knew then where he was. They'd been caught. He was but a fly encircled by the web of Zafina, the great spider at the center of all creation. He could think of no worse fate. The others, at least, would not have induced such agony by their very presence.

Luna and Sulisea were no doubt also caught, wriggling and encased in other parts of the web. They'd known the danger of using the Bridges to carry out their plan—making themselves known to Zafina each time they used one—but, without a choice, they'd done it anyway. He hoped, at least, that the rest of their team had gotten through before them.

He tried to open his mouth to speak, but nothing came but labored breath. Closing his eyes revealed the same terrible, nauseating white glow tattooed on his optic nerves. He felt his own awareness began to erode like sand in the wind. **What. Now? Where. To. Start. With. This. One.** He both felt and heard the words spoken, but at the same time saw everything flicker and begin to go out, shuddering and flickering like a candle flame.

Mmm. I'll take this one. A second voice that wasn't a voice, but seemed to come from Terry's own mind. A biting chill crept up his legs and arms. He looked down to see nothing where his feet had been, held out his hands and saw nothing there too.

He screamed, but again it fell quiet and weak. This time, when he closed his eyes he saw familiar darkness, and when he opened them again he also saw darkness Stretching endlessly in every direction as the white void had.

He felt a cool, soft surface beneath his feet, then the sensation of a vice being loosened around his torso and chest. A gray light slowly appeared in the sky, then it bled pinkish with hints of purple and deep blue. He shuffled his feet and felt the crunch of leaves, then, off in the distance, a roar so deep and furious it washed over him like a tidal wave. He froze. It was nothing like any animal he had ever heard.

A scent of moist earth drifted up to his nose, and a cold wind blew to him the last words he would hear for the next thousand years.

Shall we begin from the beginning?

Max
1872

Max felt as if he'd been running for days. Each turn around a tree, each leap over a ditch or creek was a plunge into uncertainty. It felt like a nightmare, but he knew there was no waking up from this.

The heist had gone so wrong so fast. Their fate was sealed the moment they chose the Rolling Dice as their target, and now he was pelting through the dark, pursued by gunfire. He didn't care about finding the cabin or meeting up with Steve. The only thing he cared about was getting out of the damned forest and away from the Pinkertons. Every rustle of leaves, every snap of a twig sent his heart into a flurry.

He saw the edge of the trees and for a moment hope soared within him, but when he broke through the line, he found himself in a clearing on the edge of a stream. The water was freezing as he waded into it, but he bent and scooped handfuls of it up to his mouth anyway, soaking his front. The crash of others lumbering through the trees toward him got louder, and he plunged through the water to the other side. A gunshot went off, but no bullet whizzed over him and no return fire sounded.

His head went briefly under when the ground dropped out from under him and he kicked furiously against the current, but soon he was hauling himself up the other bank, gasping too loudly. Once on dry land, he crouched and looked back, trying to see anything through the trees. Instead, what caught his eye was a body drifting with the water toward and past him. It didn't move, but her hair waved hypnotically. He couldn't make out who it was from far away, but peered through the darkness anyway, fearing he would see Sherane's wet face and hands. As she came closer, he saw that she wore an olive green shirt and brown trousers. One sleeve was rolled up to her elbow and the other hung loose and tattered. He heaved a sigh of relief.

The body gave a sudden jerk, then jostled gently side to side, hung there for a moment against something under the surface, and continued its smooth progress out of his sight. Then the sound of splashing and desperate, wet coughing.

Again, he took off, fueled by new adrenaline, and as soon as he passed back into the trees felt the tickle of tiny legs on his neck. He slapped at the insect and watched the crumpled body of a moth bounce off his shoulder. Then his next step sunk ankle-deep in a writhing black and brown mass and came up covered in bugs. The next few steps were the same, until the mass of bugs was high as his knees and they had begun to scale him. At its edges, he saw the lumpy shapes of small animals–squirrels and raccoons, even a fox–all stiff and cloudy-eyed, moving as one with the mass of bugs. He turned and ran back to the water, nearly colliding with the woman, who had climbed out of the water and was standing, motionless, pale as ice, and soaked to the bone. Her eyes were cloudy and fixed on his face, her jaw slack and unmoving.

He threw himself past her into the water, washing most of the bugs off but feeling many get caught under his clothes. His feet caught on the bottom, and he pushed his head above the water, tried to call out, but his mouth was immediately full of water and the bodies of bugs, which bounced against his teeth and held on. The top of his head began to itch. His vision went dim and his eyes started to burn, the bugs he had knocked free returning to cover his head and the hands he brought up to smack them away. He looked over and saw the woman standing at the bank, expressionless gaze still locked on him, the inky wave of more bugs pouring into the water at her feet.

Lewis

Air rushed past Lewis. He put his hands out, trying to catch himself on something, but nothing came. He continued to free fall through the dark until he splashed down into icy cold water. The shock made him go rigid, the sensation of thousands of tiny needles piercing every inch of his skin. He fought to regain the use of his limbs and flailed toward the surface, trying to direct himself across the current and toward the stream.

Eventually, when he almost couldn't bear to hold his breath any longer, his hands found a rocky ledge and he was able to haul himself out of the water and onto a precarious shelf of rock.

"Sam!" He cupped stiff hands around his mouth and called into the darkness. "Sam!" Only echoes returned.

He waited a few seconds and tried again. "Sam!" as loud as he could.

"Here!" came a faint voice.

"Sam! Ov-over here!" He reached a hand out over the water, waving it back and forth.

"Keep–keep t-t-talking." Sam's voice was closer.

"Over here!"

A hand caught awkwardly against his foot. Then he was able to get ahold of the back of Sam's sodden shirt and haul him out of the water. They sat for a moment, shivering and breathing heavily.

Lewis tried to stand, raising his arms over his head to avoid hitting it, and found that the ceiling of the cave was too high to touch, and he could stretch out his arms and take several steps before he met the wall.

"There." He felt his way back to Sam and pulled him away from the water, then tried to direct his gaze toward a tiny star of light far in the distance. It pulsed faintly. "Th–that's definitely sunlight, right?" Some of his old optimism was back, but it mixed with panicked doubt. They'd fallen so far–he doubted they were that lucky.

He tried to step toward it, but as they felt their way along the ledge, they found that it ended a few feet in front, and the only way forward was the river.

Sam gripped his shoulder. "Few-fewer obstacles in the water. J-just don't get pulled under."

They lowered themselves back into the icy river, Lewis silently cursing whatever had brought them there. They both coughed and spluttered, struggling to keep their heads above water as the current took them both away, but nothing stopped or slowed them down, and soon the water slowed and became shallow, and the growing light allowed them to make each other out across the surface.

They trudged through the now waist-high water for a while longer and then crawled heavily onto a sandy bank before the river made a switch-turn and streamed off into deeper darkness. After another moment to catch their breaths and rub feeling back into their limbs, they got up and continued toward the light on dry land. Soon, it was bright enough that Lewis could see the shadows of carvings along the wall, and went to run his fingers over them, trying to make out their shapes.

"Come on, man!" Sam yanked at the back of his shirt, weariness evident in his voice.

"Okay, okay, fine." He let himself be pulled away, but still squinted through the darkness to try and read what they passed.

Finally, they reached the mouth of the tunnel, and sunlight beamed through the opening to warm them. Anticipation surged through Lewis, and he began to run toward it, Sam close behind.

They climbed up a small pile of stones and dirt to reach the opening and winced, shielding their eyes as they climbed out onto the grass.

Once outside, they could hear the rumble of a waterfall and the calling of birds.

Sam sat slumped for a long moment, massaging his eyes and temples. Lewis got up, ignoring the burning of his limbs as they re-warmed, and found that they were at the edge of a valley in a patch of mountainside too rocky for large trees to grow. He clambered up a large rock and caught a glimpse of the bottom of the valley, where the vague shape of fences and the tops of buildings made a wave of deja vu wash over him. In the distance, the hills rolled peacefully away from the mountain and the scent of pine needles calmed his confusion. They were free, and it had been hard-won indeed.

From there, he let Sam take the lead, and together they clambered down the mountainside, over a barely-running creek, from pine trees to oaks and ash.

"The farm." Sam suddenly said, looking through a gap in the trees to a graying, overgrown farmhouse

"What?" Lewis came up behind him to look too. Sure enough, there were the log walls and the half-high stone wall along the path to the barn. As they walked through it, they found toppled fences, overgrown thatches of weeds where the gardens and fields had been, and the collapsed barn dotted with tall, healthy thornbushes. Everything was exactly where Lewis remembered

it, with the same number of steps from the the
cabin's bottom step to the edge of the barn's
now-flat roof

"Couldn't be." Lewis heard himself say.
Sam half-climbed through a large hole in the
cabin wall and came out with a rag clenched in his
fist. He held it up, and Lewis saw one of the shirts
they'd been given when they first arrived.

"Plants don't just spring up like that." Sam
said, mouth set into a firm line.

Epilogue.
1861

The stars above were bright and cold, glittering like shattered glass. Kendall lay motionless beneath them, her body aching, her mind a fog of half-formed thoughts and regret. The darkness and chill scared her, but didn't haunt as much as the hunger that gnawed at her belly. She felt faint with it, dulled, her normally precise thoughts dimmed and scattered.

Two days ago—was it two? Three? She had fled Emerald Ranch, choking on fear, thinking of nothing but safety from the gunfire behind. Observe. Document. Extract. But it had all gone wrong. The world they emerged into was sharper and more ruthless than they could have ever been prepared for. So much had been lost to history, scrubbed and sterilized as it was recorded in their history books. With every painful step, the mountain had stripped away any excitement or awe she had once had for the mission. Every scrape, every danger, every pang of hunger had rubbed her raw.

Eventually, she'd gotten desperate and disoriented enough. She'd thought the berries safe. She'd forgotten that mushrooms often had lookalikes, or her education had been faulty all along. She'd been wracked with cramps and fever, had stumbled as if drunk through the dark, helpless as a newborn.

It was almost a relief when she fell. She couldn't feel her legs. Her arms didn't move to catch her. The world faded to a haze and the scent of dirt and leaves made her gag as the stars began to disintegrate. She thought of home, the hum of her grow lights and aquaponics trays. Oliver and Eva, Mundus, and the Dawn were the last things she carried with her into the dark.

She woke to warmth and pain. A fabric ceiling flapped gently in a breeze. Her lips were dry and cracked, her tongue swollen.

"She's awake," a voice said.

It was a woman's voice, somewhere in the direction of the fire. Low and wary. Soft. Kendall tried to turn her head to look and felt it click painfully and the muscles strain.

A woman sat across the fire, her face bathed in its light.

"Don't move yet," the woman said. "You're safe."

Safe. Kendall let her eyes close. She tried to remember what safe felt like.

"She was right where you'd said she would be." The voice came again, still soothing.

"Excellent. Kendall? A dark shape blocked the light of the fire. "Are you okay?""

A memory made her open her eyes. It took a long time to see his face clearly, but when she did, she felt a weight lift off of her. She could only stare. He looked so different—broader shoulders, rough clothes and beard, but the same eyes. She summoned the strength to speak, her throat rough like sandpaper.

"Von?"

ABOUT THE AUTHOR

Grey Gardener lives just outside of Nashville. Inspiration? The motives, mysteries of humanity and the secrets hidden in history. When not writing, Grey Develops Software, he is a Husband and Father and plays chess in the form of Tekken.

www.ingramcontent.com/pod-product-compliance
Lightning Source LLC
Chambersburg PA
CBHW020147310726
48970CB00006B/2046